JOHN HORSE
FLORIDA'S FIRST FREEDOM FIGHTER

John Horse

Betty Turso
Edited by James A. Simone, Ph.D.

Copyright © 2014 Betty Turso

All rights reserved.

ISBN-13:
978-1502548900

ISBN-10:
1502548909

DEDICATION

Dedicated to the memory of my mother
whose spirit pushed the completion of this work
and to my dear friend Addis
whose spirit was and is the muse.

Preface

The Florida Wars spanned forty-two years from eighteen seventeen to eighteen fifty-eight with the Second Seminole War being the bloodiest and the most costly of the Indian Wars. It lasted seven years with Congress allocating more than thirty million dollars in an effort to control Florida. This war was a direct result of the Indian Removal Act of eighteen thirty which ordered all Indians to move west of the Mississippi onto reservations. However, the Florida Wars were about much more than displacement and relocation. They were about slavery.

As a result of the Peace of Paris treaty of seventeen eighty-three, Spain regained control of Florida from the British. Spain continued to honor its Edict of sixteen ninety-three which stated that any male slave on an English plantation who escaped to Spanish Florida would be granted freedom provided he joined the militia and became a Catholic. As a result, plantation owners in the southern states of the newly independent United States began losing their enslaved African workers. Slaveholders and slave raiders pursued fugitives on Spanish territory in attempts to capture and return their "property" to their respective owners. The Seminoles, literally "Separatists", Lower Creek Indians who fled south to Florida to escape the Creek Wars in Georgia and Alabama, gave the runaway slaves refuge and accepted them into their tribes. These "Separatists" had merged with the remnants of the tribes indigenous to Florida and became known as the Seminoles. The First Seminole War in eighteen seventeen began over attempts by U.S. authorities to recapture runaway black slaves living among Seminole bands. Under General Andrew Jackson, U.S. military forces invaded the area, scattering the villagers, burning their towns, and seizing Spanish-held Pensacola and St. Marks. As a result, in eighteen nineteen Spain was induced to cede its Florida territory to the United States under the terms of the Adams-Onis Treaty.

The Black Seminoles tended to keep communities separate from the red Seminoles but they were closely tied with intermarriages and mixed race children. They were considered slaves of the Seminoles but the relationship was not one of servitude rather it was one of cooperation. Some historians have even suggested that the term "slave" was a moniker to protect the Black Seminoles from the slavers preying on black populations. After all, if a Black Seminole is the 'legal' slave of a free Seminole, then no outside claim against the slave can be legitimized. The Black Seminoles' yearly contributions of livestock and crops to the chief seemed to be the only demand. The bond between these groups became even stronger when united against a common enemy—The U.S. Federal Government in Washington and its policy regarding the Indian Removal Act—and the Black Seminoles emerged as leaders in the war effort.

In eighteen seventeen, General Andrew Jackson led his army into Florida thus beginning the First Seminole War. Spain quickly ceded Florida to the U.S. and negotiations began with the Seminoles for removal. The time between the First and Second Seminole Wars was replete with broken promises, broken treaties, and deceit on the part of Washington. The U.S. Government pushed and the Seminoles pushed back. After years of negotiations, it was clear to the Seminoles that a fight could not be averted and they prepared for war.

The Seminoles engaged in guerilla warfare resulting in the U.S. Army walking into ambush after ambush. As soon as the cannon signaled a bayonet charge the Seminoles melted back into the swamps where the Army could not follow. These tactics resulted in countless U.S. casualties and few Seminole ones. By the time General Thomas Sydney Jesup took over command of the Florida War in eighteen thirty-six, the Army was weary and the Seminoles were starving from being kept on the move. Jesup was Washington's last hope. Jackson had gone through all his generals. He wrote, "I have tried all the Generals, and Genl (sic.) Jesup is now there . . . I hope he will finish this unfortunate business."

Until this point most of the victories were clearly Seminole; however Jesup engaged in the war on Seminole terms and began turning the tide. He did show a grasp of the situation that the others had missed when he argued, "this, you may be assured, is a negro, not an Indian war; and if it be not speedily put down, the south will feel the effect of it on their slave population before the end of the next season."

The Generals begged Jackson to give up the Florida War, the land good for nothing but alligators, insects, and Indians but he would not partly because of the money already spent and partly because of pressure from the southern Democrats. Black Seminole leaders emerged from the fray. Abraham, advisor to Micanopy, head chief of the Seminoles; John Horse, sub chief to Cowokoci, nephew of Micanopy; and John Caesar, slave of Emathla, are the most prominent. The Black Seminoles added much to the war effort. They were literate in several languages including English. They easily moved in and out of the slave population on the east coast of Florida recruiting soldiers and sparking the largest slave revolt in U.S. history. Moreover this war set the precedent for Abraham Lincoln to free the slaves in the Emancipation Proclamation January first, eighteen sixty-three.

The Seminoles, escaped from Fort Marion (Castillo de San Marcos) made their last big stand against the U.S. Military on the northern shores of Lake Okeechobee, Christmas day of eighteen thirty-seven. Colonel Zachary Taylor, who later became the twelfth president of the United States, led the troops. The only problem was the Seminoles were waiting for them. In fact they had prepared the battlefield to funnel the U.S. Army right into the sites of their sharpshooters perched in the trees. It didn't end well for Taylor that day. From here, the battle limped east to the Loxahatchee River and the site of the final two battles of the war. The war dragged on after these battles but for all intents and purposes, it was over. The Seminoles never surrendered and never signed a peace treaty. Many were bribed into emigration with payments as high as five thousand dollars and many stayed in Florida where they remain today.

Turso

One

"John Horse," cried his mother. "We must leave." John Horse was alarmed at the terror in his mother's voice. Friends and neighbors in a panic were running around Payne's Prairie, John Horse's home on the Alachua Savanna in central Florida, packing what could be carried and abandoning what could not. Elders were shouting orders. The cook fires smoldered as they fled. John Horse lingered watching the smoke. He was too young to comprehend and yet somehow he knew the smoke represented the end of life as he had known it. His life from this point forward would be dominated by dealings with the invading white Americans. Gunshots rang through the Florida savanna; braves were fighting on the opposite shore holding off General Andrew Jackson's army so the women and children could escape through the scrub and into the swamps where the white soldiers would not, could not follow. John Horse ran to catch up to his mother careful not to break the eggs his mother had charged him with carrying.

He protested. "But this is our home. What about our lodge?"

"Our home is where we can live together peacefully and remain free. That is no longer here. The white people will probably burn it after we escape."

"But it is a good shelter," John Horse exclaimed bewildered. He did not understand a people that would destroy for no reason. "Why would they do that?"

"Hurry now. There is no time. If a white man captures you, he will make you a slave. He will take you away and I will never see you again. White men are very mean to their slaves. They beat them and starve them. We must go. We can talk later. Be very quiet now."

At the time, the United States was young—just forty-one years old—and Spain controlled Florida. This bothered not only the United States founding fathers, Thomas Jefferson in particular, but the southern democrats who were losing their slave population to Florida. They petitioned the U.S. Government to do something about this and in response General Andrew Jackson, who later became the seventh President of the United States, led his army into Florida. The year was eighteen-seventeen and thus began the First Seminole War.

John Horse was five years old.

So John Horse, a mere child, held his two eggs and ran to catch his mother. She lifted him onto their horse packed with their belongings. He didn't complain. He ignored the weariness in his shoulders from holding the eggs away from his body protecting them for their dinner. He held them high when they waded through the swampy water. He wondered, "What is a white person? Why had they come? Why did they want to take him from his home?" He did not understand. The gun shots grew fainter as they traveled south. By nightfall as the baggage train travelled deep into the scrub, they could not hear them at all.

Two

When John Horse was twelve he was living in his father's village on Thlonoto-sassa Lake not far from Tampa Bay. His father was a chief. He was a good father and taught John Horse how to fish and hunt. Life was generally peaceful but with constant conversations about the white man, about moving or not moving the tribe far away, about an impending war that may or may not be avoided. He spent his days exploring the woods and wilderness careful not to encounter white slave hunters. He was very skilled at sneaking up on animals. Light-footed, he moved through the scrub never making a mark in the dead leaves, twigs, and cypress needles that blanketed the forest floor. He sneaked up on deer and rabbit and raccoon. He knew to stay downwind so his prey did not detect his presence and flee. He easily captured turtles hiding in burrows. His mother was very proud of her only son and the brave he was becoming.

"John Horse," begged his mother. "Don't go near the white fort. Please stay away from there. I will scratch you with the bear claw if you do not." Every lodge had a bear claw used to discipline the children. It was the duty of the mother to punish the children. John Horse's mother was gentle and John Horse rarely was scratched.

He had heard his mother and he understood her concern but John Horse was very curious about white people. He had seen a few from afar but not up close. He wondered about the people that made him flee as a small child. Who were they? Why did they come here? One day when John Horse was out hunting gopher turtles, he found himself near Fort Brooke. He stood in the woods unseen from the fort for a long time watching the movements of the white soldiers. With colorless skin, they looked sickly pale, and their ashen skin frightened him. Slowly he moved closer. The soldiers paid him no mind as they told each other jokes and laughed a lot. Then one tall lanky soldier with hair the color of straw waved him closer.

"Indian, come 'ere," he hollered. John cautiously moved closer. "What's you doing there?

"Yer not gonna scalp us are ya?" another soldier hollered. All the soldiers laughed. The wide-eyed John Horse just stared at the soldiers. He wasn't sure what to do. He felt he should run, but he was glued to the spot unable to move. He was half-afraid if he turned to run; they would chase him or worse shoot him. He felt they were laughing at him. He didn't think he'd done anything funny. He was confused.

"What's you got in that bag?" asked one man who was cooking a dark brown liquid over a small fire. The fire put out a lot of smoke for its size. John Horse stared at it and wondered if white people knew the right way to make a fire so it cannot be detected by outsiders. The Seminole fires are small and last an entire day. He wondered about the black drink; it was the same color as the drink that he was to drink at the next green corn ceremony, the ceremony where he would become a warrior. *It doesn't smell the same,* thought John Horse. He pondered about the white men. They were not wearing soldier's clothing. The men wearing the soldiers clothing were in a different place from these men.

Finally John Horse replied, "Gopher turtles." John Horse knew some English. His mother had taught it to him. It was the English of the plantations in the south of the United States.

"Whoa, take him to Colonel Brooks," another said. The men all laughed.

"You wanna sell those turtles? Colonel Brooks would pay a pretty price for 'em."

John Horse shrugged his shoulders. He was not sure how to react. He had not intended to sell the turtles; he intended to eat them. *Were these strange men tricking me?*

"Andrew," yelled the lanky yellow-haired one to a man inside the fort. "Take this Injun to Colonel Brooks. He's got gopher to sell."

A black man appeared and motioned John Horse to follow. John Horse wasn't sure what to do but Andrew's black skin color disarmed his fears; he didn't think a black man would trick him. It was the white men he was taught not to trust.

John Horse was a maroon— half African and half Seminole Indian. He was tall and wiry and had long straight hair and a deep black complexion with a hint of red undertones. He felt odd walking among the white men in the fort, but he followed Andrew nonetheless.

"What's your name?" Andrew asked as they walked.

"John Cawaya."

"That's Muskogee for horse," said Andrew.

"Yessir," said John Horse. "Do you speak my language?"

"I know just a few words," he said. He sized up John Horse.

"So John Horse, have you ever dealt with white men before?"

"No. Never even saw one up close until now. I saw them from a distance when I was small and had to run from them. They attacked my village."

"Well, be very respectful. Be very humble. It ain't right, but most of these men come from states where they have slaves and they expect black men to behave in certain ways. It'd be dangerous if you didn't."

John Horse listened but made no comment. *Who were these people that came to my land and expected me to act in certain ways?* John Horse had listened at council for years sitting just outside the circle occupied by the chiefs. He heard his father argue against removal. He heard Osceola threaten his own people if they talked of removal. *Why would these people want the Seminoles to move far away?* It didn't make sense to John Horse and now walking through the fort following Andrew he felt a little panic like maybe he had made a serious mistake by being there. His mother's words ran through his head. "Don't go near the white fort. Please stay away from there." *Why didn't I listen?* The threat of the bear claw did not frighten him much. His mother rarely scratched very deeply with it. He had gotten deeper scratches from the thorns on the lime trees. His mother was a gentle woman and he tried not to disappoint her. She rarely punished her children, but as the mother of his lodge it was her right to discipline as needed.

"Stay here a minute," Andrew said. He went into a door while John Horse stood outside. He thought of running but there were many men between him and the fort gate. He heard Andrew through the door.

"Colonel, there's an Indian boy here with terrapin. Are you interested?"

"Interested? Of course I'm interested! Send in the boy," the colonel replied.

Andrew motioned John Horse to enter the door.

"John Horse, this is Colonel Brooks. Show him what you have."

John Horse turned his bag over, and two gopher turtles tumbled onto the Colonel's desk. They were large and meaty. They clawed at the papers on the desk. The scratching made John Horse a little nervous. *Did I do the wrong thing?*

"Fine specimens," the Colonel said. John Horse relaxed. He could tell Colonel Brooks longed to have the turtles. "How much for these two turtles?" asked the colonel.

At first John Horse didn't know what to say. He never thought of selling turtles. He eyed the colonel growing more confident and judged what he thought he could ask.

"Two bits," he said not at all sure what two bits was.

The colonel reached into his pocket and flipped a twenty-five cent coin to John Horse; he caught it in midair.

"I could use more of these. Do you think you could bring me a couple every day?"

John Horse nodded.

"Great. Andrew, put these in the pen out back. When there's enough, we'll have a feast and invite the officers." Andrew took the terrapin from the desk and motioned John Horse to follow. John Horse followed Andrew out back and watched him put the turtles into a pen of rails.

"Now, you come back every day with more and he'll pay you two-bits every time."

John Horse nodded and ran into the forest. He was anxious to leave the fort and excited to show his father his quarter. The tribe was collecting and saving all the white man's money they could acquire in order to purchase more shot and powder. They were anticipating war at some point in the future, and they wanted to be ready. John Horse felt very grown-up as he ran. He was contributing to the future safety of the tribe. He felt proud.

Three

John Horse went to the lodge he shared with his mother, his step father, and his sister Juana. He was smiling.

"What have you been up to John Horse?" his mother asked. John Horse grinned. He held out his hand showing his mother his quarter.

"Where did you get that?"

"At the white fort."

"Oh John Horse." His mother's voice expressed concern.

"I was inside. I met the chief. He paid me this for two gophers, and he wants more."

"Oh John Horse, I'm afraid for our safety. I could never return to a life with no freedom."

"This will save the lives of Indians," his stepfather added. "We need all the white man's money we can get."

John Horse smiled. He hugged his mother and took his coin to show his father, the chief of the village. He found him sitting in council with other elders. They were discussing the white fort and whether or not the tribe should move father south into the Everglades. John Horse sat a respectable distance from the circle staring at his father and grinning.

Finally, when the talk was winding down, the chief said, "What is it John Horse? Why are you sitting there grinning?"

John Horse held out his hand with his coin resting on his palm. He saw the surprise in his father's eyes turn to pride.

"Where did you get that?"

"I've been to the white fort. I met the leader. He bought gophers from me."

Suddenly everyone was asking him questions.

"What is it like?" asked one.

"What do they do in there?" asked another.

The council was waiting for John Horse to speak and for the second time today, he felt very grown up. "They are just sitting around. Some are scraping their faces. Others are cleaning their guns. Some are sleeping. They make jokes and laugh a lot."

"Hmp," they collectively replied. They didn't expect that.

Four

The next day, John Horse went hunting for gopher turtles. Only he couldn't find any. The turtles were hiding on this day. *Maybe they don't want to feed the white people. Maybe they don't want them here on their land any more than we want them.* He searched and located the burrows the turtles dig and hide in. He probed the underground holes with a long stick and he found nothing. Sometimes the turtles are as deep as thirty feet, and John Horse knew this. It was easier to find the turtles when they surfaced to eat the sweet grasses and berries that grow on the savannah. He searched all the way to the fort. He was out behind the kitchen when he spied the pen of rails and the turtles he had sold the day before. He had an idea.

He was so proud the day before when he showed the Chiefs his money. He felt important when they listened to his account of the fort. For this reason he wanted to take more money back to his tribe. The only problem was he didn't find any turtles this day. He reached into the pen and removed the two turtles. He placed them in his bag and went into the fort. He found Andrew and showed him his turtles.

"Very nice," said Andrew indicating that John Horse should go with him. They went to Colonel Brooks' quarters.

"What do you have there young man?" asked Colonel Brooks.

"Just two gopher," John Horse replied. He put the turtles on the table and Andrew took them.

"You know I'll take as many as you can bring. You don't have to bring only two."

"Yes," said John Horse. "They was hidin' today. It's too hot and I guess they's deep underground."

"True," agreed Colonel Brooks. "Do your best."

"Yessa," John Horse replied. He was anxious to leave in case Andrew noticed the two turtles from yesterday missing. He took his two bits and quickly fled the fort.

"What's your hurry?" Andrew yelled after him.
John Horse waved and ran on. As he ran, his anxious mood gave way to a lighter almost giddy one; he was amused at how easily he had fooled the white man. He entered his mother's lodge laughing.

"What is so funny?" asked his mother. John Horse held out his new quarter. His mother took it and put it away with the first one.

"Why are you laughing?

"I sold the white chief the same turtles that I sold him yesterday."

"What?" his mother said, her voice rising.

"I couldn't find any gophers today. It's too hot. So I took the two from the Colonel's pen and sold them to him again."

"John Horse, you didn't."

John Horse shook his head yes. His mother joined in his laughter. Juana, his sister ran laughing from the lodge to tell her friends. Soon the whole village knew how John Horse had duped the white chief. His mother looked on as the tribe gathered around John Horse laughing and slapping his back. She laughed with them but she felt an inkling of apprehension. She did not like her son dealing with the white men.

His father beat his chest, "My son, my son," he said. John Horse was very proud.

Everyone was happy, but his mother still worried.

The next day, John Horse so full of himself from all the attention hardly worked at finding turtles. After all, if he couldn't find any, he'd just resell the originals.

And this is what he did. And he continued to do this for the next week.

Meanwhile, Colonel Brooks was finalizing plans for an officer's dinner. The gopher turtles supplied by John Horse would be the main course.

Five

"What?" yelled Colonel Brooks. "What do you mean? There are only two turtles?"

"I'm sorry sir; I looked several times. There are only two," Andrew said calmly. He could see the agitation rising in the colonel. He saw the colonel's face turn red with anger.

The colonel stomped out to his pen of rails. He stood staring into the pen in disbelief. It was as if his mind could not comprehend that there were only two turtles in total.

"Orderly," he screamed. "Go fetch this John Horse and bring him here. That thief sold me the same two turtles again and again."

"Perhaps they escaped," said Andrew. "Or maybe someone took them." He was trying to defuse the colonel's anger. Andrew liked John Horse and didn't want to see him hurt. Secretly he admired John Horse's bravado.

"You didn't notice there were no turtles each day?"

"No sir, I just plunked them in there. They like to burrow so I just thought they were under the leaves or something. I suppose they could have burrowed themselves out of the pen."

"Nonsense." Colonel Brooks huffed and stomped back to his quarters. The orderly mounted his horse and rode off in the direction of the Seminole village. He took two soldiers with him in case of trouble. He took his time, keeping his horse at a slow trot. He was in no hurry to get there. He was in no hurry to attempt to take an Indian boy from his village; he wasn't sure how he might be received by the chiefs. The soldiers rode along wondering how they would handle the situation when they came upon the village.

"I'm looking for John Horse," said the orderly to children playing at the edge of the village. One boy understood the name and pointed to the trees where John Horse stood alone. The orderly was so relieved that he was grinning when he met John Horse. "Hey boy, I've been looking for you."

"Me? Why?"

"Yep, you. You're John Horse, right? Colonel Brooks would like to see you. Come on along with me."

Since he was grinning, John Horse didn't suspect anything was wrong. He was actually feeling a little full of himself. He was on his way to resell the two turtles. He rode along next to the man silently. The two soldiers followed. He didn't know what to say to a white man. He tried to think of something but his mind remained blank. He wondered why they had come for him. The orderly was so relieved that he was almost laughing. He chuckled to himself every time he looked at John Horse. Soon they were at the fort.

"Put your horse up there," the orderly told John Horse. He pointed to a rail where several horses were tied. "Come with me."

John Horse finally mustered one word. "Why?"

"I don't know. Something about turtles." When John Horse heard this, he turned to go. The orderly stopped him and shoved him toward the Colonel's quarters. "No, git on in there," he ordered.

Colonel Brooks saw John Horse. "There you are you little thief." John Horse hung his head and looked down. "You sold me turtles every day this week and there are only two. What do you have to say for yourself?" he asked. He was fuming. "I want to know what you thought you were doing. I have a mind to throw you in the brig. I have a mind to tan your hide!"

John Horse stole a glance at the colonel. He tried to figure out if he was in danger. He hung his head and said, "I'm sorry. I couldn't find any gophers, and I didn't want to disappoint you."

"What?"

"I planned to fill the pen before you noticed. You were so happy with the gophers that you gave me extra food. My mother needed extra rations because we were hungry."

This excuse disarmed Colonel Brooks. His anger melted. "Okay then," he said, feigning anger. "You will bring me two turtles for every two bits I gave you."

"Yessa," agreed John Horse.

"And an extra two for my trouble. From now on, you will be called Gopher John as a reminder of your dishonesty." He stared at John Horse sternly. "So Gopher John get out of here and go find some gophers. Now!" Then he turned to Andrew. "Andrew, give John Horse some rations for his family."

John Horse fled the room, but Andrew summoned him to follow. In the storeroom, he gave John Horse some flour and some jerky. John Horse left the fort quickly and headed home. He was a little shaken. The colonel frightened him. He was afraid he would lock him in the room with bars on the windows. If this happened, who would help his stepfather find food? The food John Horse was carrying confused him. *Why would the colonel give his family food? Why would he reward his actions?* John Horse didn't know at that point if he would replace the turtles; he had to think about it. Maybe he should just disappear and never see the white fort again. He asked his mother what should he do.

"Oh John Horse," she said. "I begged you to stay away from that fort."

"I know," John Horse answered.

"I think you should fill the man's pen with gophers so he won't come and hurt us."

"Do you think he would?"

"I don't know. I think he could if he wanted to." John Horse spent the next two weeks finding gopher turtles and putting them in Colonel Brooks' pen of rails. He would feel terrible if his family endured repercussions for his actions. When he had put a dozen gophers into the pen, he went to see Colonel Brooks.

"I filled your pen," he explained.

"Excellent," said Colonel Brooks. He laughed and stood. "Let's see." Together they went out to the pen. When the captain saw the turtles, he patted John on the back. "Very good, Gopher John," he said. "Keep bringing them. I'll take all you can get. I love gopher. Mmmm good!"

Six

John Horse spent the next few years living a rather peaceful life. The tribe went about day-to-day business in spite of the ongoing subtle and underlying threat posed from the presence of the American military. John Horse felt it too; he was aware of it. Since his entire life had been spent under this threat, he went about his life as usual. He took a wife, Susan[1], daughter of July. They had sons. John Horse was a responsible father and a good husband. He provided for his family by acquiring twenty head of cattle and grazing his herd on the savannah where he had grown up.

One day John Horse went to check on his herd. He could not find it. Puzzled, he looked in all directions. Not a cow could be seen. He checked the hoof prints in the dirt and they all headed in one direction. He followed his herd. At first he just thought something spooked them and they all went together away from the perceived danger but the hoofs prints showed the cows were not running but rather they were walking. John Horse was confused. Who could have stolen his herd? Certainly no Seminole. Seminole respected each other's brands. John Horse's brand was clearly marked on each of his cattle.

John Horse tracked his cattle until he came upon a camp of American soldiers. Approaching the camp cautiously, he observed a man sitting on a rock guarding a pen of cattle.

"Hello," said John Horse. "I'm John Cawaya."

"Whitney's my name. What can I do for you?"

"Well, it seems you are guarding a herd of cattle that includes twenty cows that belong to me. See there? That's my brand."

"Oh. I rounded up these cattle from Tokope Keliga."

"Yes," said John Horse. "That is my home. That is where I keep my herd."

"Well, you see," said Whitney. "I was just doing my job. The United States Army has the right to confiscate supplies for the army. It's legal."

"That doesn't seem quite right to me. Indians call that stealing."

"We got an army to feed," Whitney defended his position.

"You're entitled to be paid for them."

"I would rather have my cattle. It's food for my people." He thought about it, looked around and realized there was no way he could take them from this large force of soldiers. That was one thing the Seminole never did; they never engaged in a losing battle if it could be avoided. Resigned, he asked, "Where can I get paid?"

"Just go file a claim with Colonel Graham's orderly. He's right there inside the camp. See that man right there?"

"The one carrying the blankets?"

"Yea, that's him. Go talk to him," Whitney instructed.

John Horse dismounted and tied his horse to a tree. He walked up to the man with the blanket.

"I understand that you will pay me for my cows that you have penned up over there," John Horse explained to the man.

"Can you prove they are yours?"

"That's my brand. Everyone knows that is a Seminole brand."

"Okay. We just need to fill out some paperwork here." The man had a makeshift desk made from two barrels with a board resting on top of them. He sat behind the desk and motioned John to sit in the other chair. "So what is your name?"

"John Cawaya, Seminole," John Horse replied. "The army sometimes calls me Gopher John. I'm well-known to Colonel Brooks."

"All right. I'll note that here in the explanation box. We just need to settle on a price. I'll send these papers to Washington. After the U.S. Government approves your claim, you can get your money."

"How do I do that?" asked John Horse.

"Just check back periodically."

"How often?" he asked.

"Oh, every now and then, maybe once a month."

John Horse didn't feel good about leaving without his cattle but he couldn't take them from a whole army by himself. At least they acknowledged that they took them. He would talk to the chiefs and see what they think he should do. For now, he headed home. He knew where his cattle were and there wasn't anything he could do about it at the moment.

Seven

When John Horse arrived in camp, the men were in council. He quickly slid into the circle and listened.

"We're meeting with General Wiley Thompson in seven days at Fort King. He speaks for some great white father they call Jackson who is evidently their chief." said Cowokoci. Cowokoci is called Wild Cat by the white men, and is the son of the great and honorable Chief Emathla also known as King Phillip (not to be confused with Charlie Emathla). Cowokoci is also nephew of Micanopy and the likely heir to be the main chief after Micanopy is gone. Cowokoci is John Horse's best friend. They vowed to fight together to the death if necessary.

"Great white father?" responded Osceola. "What makes him great? Does he come to talk? Does he come to hear our talk? Is this respect?" Osceola embodied the spirit of resistance. He was a Red Stick Creek Indian. His father was a white man from Scotland named Powell. When he was a boy and he and his mother were escaping the Creek Wars, they were traveling with white relatives. For this reason they were allowed to pass to Florida. How different might things have been had Osceola been stopped at the border as a boy and sent west. The white soldiers often called Osceola by his father's name, Powell, which was an insult to him because Osceola did not acknowledge his white heritage; he considered himself Indian. Even though he had no hereditary right to become a chief, his deeds on the battlefield would make him a respected war chief.

"War will be costly for us in both property and lives. Let us hear his talk," advised Micanopy, the head chief. "We do not have to agree with this father." Micanopy had grown old and fat. He was lazy and did not want to engage in war with the U.S. Army. He was Chief but his tribe as a whole did not want to leave Florida. Micanopy did not want to leave Florida either but he would have preferred leaving to fighting.

"We will not agree to leave," said Ote Emaltha, another chief. "But if we listen and appear to consider their ideas, we can get supplies from the white fort."

"Our people are hungry," added Micanopy. "Besides we are not ready for an extended war. We need more time. Talks give us more time."

"We must be honest," said Holata Emathla. "Our chiefs signed a paper. This agent only wants us to honor our promise."

"When the Great Spirit tells me to go to the west, I will go. Until then, I stay. When the white man tells me to go away from my lands, I hate him. I love my home and will not go from it," said Osceola vehemently. Anger spewed with his words.

"But our chiefs did promise," said Ote Emathla.

"They did, but our chiefs did not do what we told them to do," retorted Osceola. "They did wrong. We are not obliged to honor a bad paper."

"Let us hear what the white agents have to say," advised Micanopy. "Then we will talk again. Besides even if we agree to the treaty, our twenty years is not up. If our chiefs agreed, they agreed to twenty years."

Osceola stomped off. He was angry with their talk. He would tolerate no talk of moving west. He considers anyone who would even think about it an enemy even if that person is kin.

Cowokoci pulled John Horse aside. They walked and talked. "What do you think?" asked Cowokoci.

"I don't think the white man is honest. I just came from the white camp. The soldiers have my cattle. They said they had the right to take them."

"That is not right. How are we to feed our people if they take our food?"

"He said he had an army to feed and it was legal to take my property. How can we trust anything the white man says when he can justify stealing so easily? What kind of a government justifies stealing another's food?" asked John Horse.

"I don't know. I think Osceola is right; we must destroy them and drive them from this land," replied Cowokoci.

"I agree. Let us go talk with Osceola. I think even if we agreed to go west, my family would not get there. We would be made slaves."

John Horse and Cowokoci went to Osceola. Osceola was still fuming over Holata Emathla and Ote Emathla thinking they should follow the treaty.

"Osceola, can we talk?" asked Cowokoci.

"If you are here to convince me to honor the treaty, you are wasting your time."

"No," said John. "We agree with you."

"Then you are wise."

"Yes," said John Horse. "My people can never go west. The Creeks are there, and they would sell my family and me into slavery."

"That is true. They would take my wife too," said Osceola.

"Yes. I will fight until my people are free or until I am dead," said John Horse.

Osceola nodded. "You are a good man John Horse. We will fight together to victory."

"Abraham also thinks we, Black Seminoles, are in great danger," added John Horse. "But he thinks he is safe for the time being as long as he stays near Micanopy. I don't think so."

Abraham is the respected leader of the Black Seminoles and sub-chief to Micanopy. He is a wise council for Micanopy.

"I do not think any of us are safe," added Cowokoci. "Especially the women and children. I will never cooperate with the invaders to my land, but I will go to the talk and see what they say. If they think we might leave, they will give us provisions. Our people are hungry. The soldiers have kept us on the run and we could not plant maize."

"True and they stole my cattle," said John Horse. "They owe me food."

"We should go to this meeting, Osceola," advised Cowokoci. "But we will never agree to leave. It is to our advantage to make them relax and not notice we are stockpiling gunpowder and shot. We need more time to prepare for a war we will win."

"Besides," said John Horse. "They will not relax if you are not involved in the talks. They respect and fear you Osceola."

"Perhaps," said Osceola. He pondered that thought for a moment and then he said, "I will go, but I will never leave my land. My blood will soak into this ground before I will surrender."

"Mine too," added Cowokoci. "I will win or die."

"I am in agreement," said John Horse. He did agree with Osceola. He knew he could never surrender. He would be made a slave. His mother warned him to avoid the white man from the time he was a young boy. She told horrible stories of being a slave at the hands of the white man. John Horse was a husband and a father. He had more to think of than just himself. John Horse did not sleep well the nights before the talks. He was very anxious. Even if the red Seminoles agreed to honor the treaty, he would not.

Eight

The talks and arguments continued among the Seminoles—both red and black— until finally it was time to meet the Indian Agent General Wiley Thompson.

John Horse's wife Susan waked him on the morning of the talks. She was the daughter of July, chief of Peliklakaha, a Seminole stronghold often referred to as Black Town.

"John Horse," said his wife Susan. "The men are preparing to go to the talks. John Horse," she said again gently. John Horse began to stir. He had fallen asleep late in the night, and he did not wake as he usually did with the sun.

"Thank you," he said to his wife. He rose, took the jerky Susan handed him for breakfast and went to join the men. They were arguing.

Abraham was vehement. "I will go with you," he was saying to Micanopy. "But I do not trust the white man; this could be a trick."

"We must hear what they have to say," Micanopy was saying as John Horse walked up to the group.

"Osceola has agreed to go," said John Horse. "It will be alright," he said to Abraham. Although John Horse wasn't entirely sure himself, he knew he could not make accurate judgments without looking the enemy in the face. He would observe as the white man talked. Abraham was still very concerned. He too could be taken into Southern chattel slavery like John Horse and his family. The situation was dangerous for all the Seminoles but especially so for the Black Seminoles.

"We will go," said Cowokoci. "But we will have our warriors quietly waiting in the scrub. If something goes horribly wrong, they will act."

"That is a good idea," said John Horse. "I will feel better knowing that we are not alone with the soldiers."

"This is smart thinking my nephew," said Micanopy to Cowokoci. "Abraham, do you agree?"

"Yes," he said.

Abraham spoke fluent English and often accompanied the Seminole chiefs, mainly Micanopy, as interpreter. He was much respected and his council was valued. Micanopy relied heavily on

Abraham for advice and guidance. Micanopy made decisions based on Abraham's advice.

"In fact, I think you should stay with the tribe. This will give us the excuse to say we must take this to Micanopy before we can commit. It gives us time to think."

"That sounds good. I can wait with the warriors in the scrub." Micanopy liked the idea because he didn't like confrontation. He was chief through heredity. If he had been made to work for it, he would have remained a brave. He much preferred waiting in leisure for the chiefs to return with the news of the talks. "Then, let us prepare," ordered Micanopy. The chiefs went to their lodges to dress in their finest formal clothing.

John Horse returned to his chickee. Susan was fussing with his formal clothing. She was straightening his large oversize calico shirt removing the wrinkles. She remembered when he obtained the cloth from the trading posts. He was so proud. John Horse liked to look nice and he always took care in his manner. It is respectful to the Creator to take care in appearance. That is what first made her notice him. He was so tall and proud. He wore his shirt belted at the waist and it hung to his knees. It was highly decorated with many silver ornaments and feathers. Susan had decorated his belt with glass beads that he brought home one day. She took care to line up the beads perfectly. She sewed them on when he was out hunting so she could surprise him with the finished belt when he returned home. He wore buckskin leggings with brightly colored blue scarves tied at the knees; feathers hung from the scarves. Susan helped him wind his turban around his head tightly so it would stay in place while riding. She took care to make sure his feathers were securely anchored into the turban. He wore deerskin moccasins and carried a bandoleer bag. Into the bag she put ammunition and powder. The bag was also decorated with beads and beadwork and he wore the strap crosswise over his chest. A necklace of silver crescent moon-shaped discs finished off the outfit. Susan stood back and admired him when he was dressed. John Horse always took care and today he took extra special care. He was nervous and Susan teased him to lighten his mood.

"Oh John Horse, you look very handsome. You're not looking for another wife now are you? Are there wives at the white fort?" she asked.

They laughed. He looked at his wife, his children, his sister and her children and his eyes became serious. "I have to be focused. Our freedom depends on it."

"Be careful John Horse," she said as he walked toward the group mounting horses for the journey to Fort King.

Micanopy led the entourage; they rode in silence. Each man was thinking about what would come of these talks. Each man worried that it might be a trap. When they were a half a mile from the fort, Micanopy stopped and held up his hand as a signal for the others to stop. He pointed to his left and to his right and his warriors melted into the Florida scrub. He followed the warriors into the scrub. The warriors would tie-up their horses and move closer to the fort through the dense underbrush on foot. There they would wait until it was over or until they heard a war cry. If one of the chiefs whooped loudly, they would advance on the fort.

The rest continued toward the fort. The year was eighteen thirty-four; it was springtime.

Nine

General Thompson emerged from his quarters as the Indians came into camp. He smiled and greeted the Seminole warmly. The Indians were apprehensive and fearful. They dismounted and waited. General Thompson directed the visitors to a platform in the middle of the barracks. It was large and built high off the ground to avoid snakes and other crawling things. It was out of the sun and used for soldier drills when the sun was too hot. John Horse looked around. He looked at Cowokoci. They exchanged a knowing look. The soldiers looked nervous too. Cowokoci smiled at their discomfort. John Horse worried if they were nervous about a secret plan to arrest them all. Nonetheless he was here so he would remain but keep a watchful eye focused on the nuances of the soldiers' movements. The principal chiefs sat on benches on one side. General Thompson and his officers sat on benches on the opposite side of the platform. Cudjo, a black man, was positioned in the center of the platform; he was to be the interpreter. He was a respected Black Seminole and chief and he was being paid by the U.S. Government to interpret for the army.

Agent Wiley spoke first. "I speak for our great white father, President Jackson. He cares very much for his red children. He is very disappointed that his red children are resisting emigration to the west. He feels you are morally bound to honor the treaty signed by your own chiefs." Cudjo interpreted Agent Wiley's words. He spoke in slow broken English so the exchange took a while. Everyone listened patiently as he spoke. Flies buzzed about the heads of the Indians and soldiers alike. The morning sun dispelled the night coolness from the earth. The Seminole were nervous and uncomfortable. The soldiers were sweating and wondering why they were in this hell called Florida.

Ote Emathla stepped forward to speak. "The treaty you refer to gave us twenty years in peace to live and flourish on our land. That time is not up. We understood that when twenty years was gone we would talk again. You asked us to sign a paper that said the lands in the west were good. To this we agreed. We signed a paper that said the lands were fertile, that the fruit of the land was sweet, but we warned that the lands were surrounded by hostile neighbors and we could have no peace there. Now you say we agreed to move. We only agreed that the lands were good."

General Thompson took a paper from his leather case and placed it on the table. "Here is the treaty," he said. "It has the names of your chiefs."

Charlie Emathla stepped forward to speak. "Our voice, John Hicks, was a great man. He died and left his children for us to father. His signature makes that paper sacred, but the time has not expired. When it does, we will make a new bargain."

"The great white father is disappointed. He believes you are bound to move. You were not forced to sign the paper but your own chiefs signed the paper in good faith and now as honorable men, you must go," said Thompson. He swatted at a fly. His patience was growing thin. The bead of sweat that formed on his forehead was now running down his face. He was hot and tired and wanted this over.

Charlie Emathla responded. "I am full-blooded Indian. I do not change my mind once it is set. I am a man. I live on the land where I was born. My children play on this land. If the great white father believes we are his children, why does he not see that we do not hunger for new land? We are happy on our land. My land is sacred in my heart. I believe, Agent Thompson, that you are my friend and you will understand. Talk is good."

Abiaka, chief of the Miccosukee, called Sam Jones by the soldiers, was leaning against the platform. He was not happy with the proceedings. He stomped his feet and made ferocious sounds. He was very old, born sometime around seventeen sixty. He was respected and a strong medicine man.

"Auugg," he grunted. He slapped the support post. Just as he did there was a loud crack. Everyone was startled. Before anyone could discern the source of the large cracking sound, the platform tumbled down. Seminole chiefs and U.S. Army officers alike tumbled into one great pile in the center of the broken platform; their arms and legs were flailing every which way as the men tried to disentangle themselves from the pile. General Clinch, a large rotund man, was rolling around like a pig in mud. At first the Indians were startled fearing a trap, but quickly everyone realized what happened and laughter broke out on both sides. John Horse laughed so hard tears streamed form his eyes. *How are these men a match for us? They cannot even make a platform!* The talks were adjourned for the day.

"Ha ha ha," chuckled Alligator. "Seminole platforms do not fall. General, you need building lessons from the Seminole."

"Yes," said Charlie Emathla. "You need the Seminole to stay here and teach you how to live in this land." Everyone laughed.

"We will meet in council tonight and talk again tomorrow," suggested General Thompson.

The Indians nodded in agreement. They mounted their horses, turned their backs on General Thompson, and rode from camp. They made camp a mile from the Fort. The warriors joined them. They laid skins on the ground and sat for council.

"These talks are useless," said Osceola. "The white man will not hear our side."

"They are," said Cowokoci. He stomped his foot for emphasis.

"Yes," said Micanopy. "They do seem stubborn but it is only the first day. You have made them know our feelings. We will reinforce our position tomorrow. We will tell them again how we feel."

"Do you expect any change from them?" asked Holati Mico.

"We will make our position known and then we must give General Thompson time to speak with his great white father. Then we will see. In the meantime, we will stockpile supplies needed for war." Micanopy did not want war but preparing for it placated the other chiefs for now. He just wanted to avoid turmoil.

"It is a good plan," said Abraham.

The Seminoles talked late into the night. They argued and they agreed. They surmised and thought of scenarios and argued at the outcomes of the scenarios. *If we fight, how many will die? If we go west, how many will die?* There were no easy answers and it was looking more and more like a no-win situation.

John Horse lay on his blanket and thought of the day's events. He knew that no definite answers could be known and that caused anxiety. He felt the heavy burden of war hanging over his head. He felt the responsibility he had toward his people. Abraham was getting old and tired. He knew he would be called on to lead. He knew he would accept the challenge but still he felt afraid. He was thankful he could count Cowokoci and Osceola as his friends. He felt confident that they would stand with him and never give up.

Ten

The Indians rose with the dawn. They ate, and the talks continued. The Seminoles were amused and puzzled at the soldiers' ways.

"Why do they march in groups like that?" wondered John Horse.

"It is amazing how they can stay in step and turn at once without losing a step," said Osceola.

"I see them do that for hours on end and for some reason they are very proud of being able to march together like that," added Cowokoci.

"I know," said Osceola, "but how is that maneuver useful in battle? It makes no sense to me."

"I don't know either," said Cowokoci. "It's seems like a waste of time, and it tires the soldiers. White people make no sense to me."

"Yes, but did you notice how they advance on an enemy?" asked John Horse.

"Very good that you noticed that," said Osceola. "The soldiers advance in lines. The first line fires and then lies down so the next line can fire over their heads."

"I saw that too," said Cowokoci. "It's like they are showing us how to defeat them. After the initial volley, we just shoot at the ground."

"You are smart fighters," said Osceola. John Horse and Cowokoci grinned at the compliment.

Finally it was time to return to Fort King. Talks resumed as soon as they arrived. The Indian agents were waiting for them. General Thompson was sitting at a wooden table with the Treaty of Moultrie on the table in front of him. The white man wanted the Indians to move to reservation land in the west. This treaty was an agreement to emigrate. However the conditions under which it was signed are questionable. The chiefs insist that they were tricked into signing a paper that was changed from what they thought they were signing. The U.S. Government insists they agreed to leave Florida.

The talks continued.

"As I said yesterday," said Holati Mico. "I have no enemy in the white man. We are both from the Creator. However, we must proceed carefully and with reason in these talks. We represent many people with many ideas. We must give our people time to consider their differences. We have much care and thoughtfulness for our people."

Halpatter Tustenugee known as Alligator to the soldiers added, "My talk today is the same as my talk yesterday. When twenty years from the Treaty of Moultrie have passed, we may consent to go to the west. For now we will not."

Micanopy, present on the second day because his original fears were assuaged, nodded agreement to Halpatter Tustenugee. He sat in the middle of the Seminoles looking regal and proud. He said little but he was a formidable presence as leader of the Seminole Nation.

"When our chiefs negotiated the treaty, they did not have the consent of the tribes. The people reject it," Halpatter Tustenugee continued.

General Thompson became angry. "You are not men. Men honor their word. You have no sense of fidelity or truth," he stated. When Cudjo interpreted this remark, there was uproar. Everyone yelled. The Indians spoke loudly to each other and to the agents. The regulars that had been standing quietly behind the officers became agitated and argued among themselves. General Thompson's words caused chaos. General Clinch, who had remained in the background, stepped forward. He restored order among the Indians at least temporarily.

"Honorable chiefs, I appeal to your humanity. I have troops at my disposal and will engage them if order is not restored."

His threat quieted the crowd. The Indians were not intimidated as the general thought. They were calculating. How many warriors were at their disposal? How many troops were in camp? The Indians were smart warriors. They would not engage in a fight of certain death. They would wait for an advantage before fighting General Clinch and his army.

"Who will honor the treaty?" he asked.

"I will honor the treaty as I interpret it," said Holati Mico.

This pleased General Clinch but he did not understand what the chief meant. He meant that they did not agree to go west, only to speak of it again in the future when the original twenty years was up. Seven chiefs agreed with him: Micanopy as legitimate leader of the Seminole, Ote Emathla also known as Jumper, Halpatter Tustenugee, Chief Abiaka, and Black Dirt.

General Thompson still fuming said to the remaining chiefs, "Then you are no longer chiefs." He struck through their names on his paper. "You are no longer representatives of your people."

"You cannot do that," said Ote Emaltha. "You do not pick our chiefs." The other chiefs stood in amazement at the gall of this white man disavowing their chiefs.

Angered, Osceola shook off his amazement and stepped forward. He thrust his knife into the treaty sitting on the table. "This is the only treaty I will honor. There is nothing left for words." The soldiers were stunned and did not know what to do. The generals also were dazed and in the confusion John Horse quickly mounted his horse to leave. Abraham followed. Should the white soldiers arrest them, they could be sold into slavery. John Horse did not fear that he would be enslaved for long; he would escape but it would take time and his family would be vulnerable. The Indians mounted and quickly followed. Micanopy signaled the hidden warriors to join them and they rode quickly for home.

Eleven

When they returned to Micanopy's camp, a visitor was there to talk. He had a warning from John Caesar, a Black Seminole living in the swamps south of Jacksonville. He had been gathering intelligence from the black people enslaved in the plantations along the coast. He recruited slaves to join the Seminole cause. He traded with Cubans for arms and ammunition.

"John Caesar sent me to warn you. The great white chief Jackson has ordered the army to move the Seminoles from Florida and to make them live with the Creeks."

"The Creeks will make us slaves," said Abraham. "We recently met with the Indian agent General Thompson and we told him the same."

"Yes they will," the visitor agreed with Abraham. "The Creeks are very mean to slaves. They separate families and beat men for no reason. They sell slaves to the white planters up north." The men nodded in agreement and the visitor continued. "John Caesar has been leading raids on the plantations where the great salt water meets the land. He is trying to divide the army so fewer men can attack at a time."

"That is a very good move," said Abraham. "We should divide the tribes so the army must also divide to pursue us."

"But there is safety in numbers. The more guns aimed at the white man, the more white men dead," said Cowokoci. "We must be diligent so they will give up and go back to the north from where they came."

"I don't think the white man will ever leave. The chief that orders them is not with them. It is easy to order men to fight and die when you are not with them."

"That is also true," added Abraham. "He is a coward."

"We are getting guns and ammunition from fishermen from Cuba. They will bring as much as we can buy. They bring them to a Port Charlotte in the north and white men's slaves sympathetic to our cause smuggle them south to St. Augustine. It is very dangerous work because the white chief has made it illegal for a black man to have a gun or ammunition. He hangs a black man by the neck if he catches him with a gun."

"We have been saving gold, silver, and white man's money to purchase arms," said Chief Micanopy. He had been listening quietly to Abraham and the visitor talk.

"John Horse, go back with this man to St. Augustine. Talk to enslaved men; recruit them to fight with us. Purchase all the ammunition you can with our money. Soon we are to meet again with Wiley Thompson. He speaks for their chief Jackson. If that does not go well, I want to be ready for war. See if Cowokoci can go with you." Micanopy was bending to the pressure of his chiefs and his advisor, Abraham. He was facing the idea that he must fight to rid his people of the curse of the white man. He still hoped for a way out of war but he knew he must be ready in any case. Not to prepare could be suicide.

John Horse nodded. His dark skin allowed him to slip into St. Augustine and listen to people talk. He could find out important things. The white man, thinking he was a slave, paid little attention to him. Even though he did not like to wear white man's clothes because they were uncomfortable and tight, binding his movements, he was proud to be given such an important job. He would fight for freedom to the death. He loved his family and did not want to see his sons enslaved. This was more important to him than even his own freedom. He went to his lodge to prepare to leave.

"Susan," he said to his wife, "I am going north for ammunition. We must be ready to fight in case talks with white man do not go well."

Susan nodded. "The talks will not go well," she said quietly almost to herself. She did not want John Horse to go but she knew he must. She knew the freedom of her children depended on John Horse and the warriors. As a woman of the tribe, she would do whatever was necessary. She quickly prepared a bundle of food for John Horse's journey. She swiftly hugged him and kissed him good-bye. Indians did not often show affection in public but she was overcome with emotion. John Horse laughed and returned her hug. His heart was warm for his wife and family.

In the meantime, Micanopy had gathered some of the tribe's gold and silver and gave it to John Horse who placed it in a pouch that he tied around his waist. Should he get separated from his horse, he would retain the tribe's fortune. When it was decided that

Cowokoci would go with him, John Horse divided the money and gave half to his friend to carry. The party of three trotted from the village. The tribe watched until they were out of sight. Susan wiped a tear from her eye. She already missed her husband but even more she feared for his safety. She could not imagine life without him but in these harsh times a long life was not guaranteed.

The ride to St. Augustine was an easy two days. The main danger was to avoid the slave hunters and army scouts. The men rode quietly through the scrub and did not make a fire at night. They ate salted beef for dinner. They slept only a few hours, anxious to reach the relative safety of their destination. Once the horses were rested, they resumed their journey. Late afternoon of the second day they reached John Caesar's camp in the swamps south of St. Augustine. John Caesar greeted them warmly.

He put a cow skin on the ground and invited John Horse and Cowokoci to join him. His wife brought them food and drink. They ate fry bread made from the wild coonti plant and taal-holelke, a boiled cabbage from the cabbage palm. Once the three had eaten, they talked. Chiefs and warriors generally eat in silence and conduct their business after the meal is done.

"I am trying to divert some of the army from the main Seminole tribe by attacking the plantations south of St. Augustine," said John Caesar.

"The chiefs appreciate your efforts," said Cowokoci.

John Horse nodded. He looked around and saw a mostly deserted camp. "Where are your warriors?" he asked.

John Caesar responded, "Most of my men are slaves from the plantations. Many spend the days where the white owners can see them and then join me on the raids at night."

"That is very good," said John Horse. "And food is not an issue in this case. Our people are low on food. We cannot stay in one place long enough to plant our maize. We need as many warriors as we can get so we can drive the white man away and go back to our comfortable life of abundant food."

"Yes. That is why I would like you to spend a couple of days talking to the plantation slaves," said John Caesar. "Tell them of your free life. Convince them to join us."

"I would be honored," said John Horse.

"Now you must rest," said John Caesar. "Tonight we will raid."

Later that night John Horse and Cowokoci awoke to many voices. The enslaved men from the surrounding plantations were gathering in camp. John Horse and Cowokoci rose and joined them. John Caesar made introductions.

"This is John Horse, Black Seminole leader, and Cowokoci, nephew of Micanopy, Great Chief of the Seminole. They will join us tonight. John Horse is a free black man; he will tell you of his free life.

"It is an honor to meet you," said one of the men. "Tonight is a good night for the raid. Most of the white men are in a meeting with the army chief. They went to demand protection for their plantations to the south," said another man. He pointed to the south as he spoke.

"This is good information," replied John Caesar.

"Yes," said another. "We should start south and work up to the Godfrey plantation." All agreed and the men prepared to leave.

John Horse observed John Caesar as they rode. He was a serious man and a good leader. He was smart to cause disruption here in the north and make the army divide. *The men meeting with the white soldier chief are demanding more protection,* he thought, *they are afraid. John Caesar has them scared.* John Horse longed to live a peaceful life with his family. He wanted to sit in the sun and watch his children play like he did as a boy. His children had very little time for playing. He could not allow them to explore the land. *Mother Nature is a good teacher,* he thought. *My children do not get to explore her. It is too dangerous to let them out of sight.* In camp, the children were made to stay close. If the tribe had to move quickly, there would be no time to find a wandering child. Besides, it was dangerous. The white chief ordered his army to capture every Indian that could be found, women and children alike. John Horse longed for the time when he explored in relative safety. He could never allow his son to enter the white camp with gopher to sell like he did as a child. His heart ached for his children. John Horse did not like war. He did not like killing. He was a warrior because it was his duty as father and husband to protect his family. His family would never be slave to the white man as long as he drew breath.

The war party approached the last plantation. John Caesar held his hand into the air to halt the party. "John Horse, Cowokoci," he said. "Lead five warriors to the south. We will wait five minutes and when you hear our call attack from the south. We will come from many directions at once."

John Horse nodded and turned his horse south. The party had just gotten into place when they heard John Caesar's war cry.

"Whoop, Whoop, Whooooop," screamed John Caesar. Many voices joined and they attacked the house. John Horse kicked his horse spurring him faster. He fired his rifle as he rode. He shot at the house. He heard his rifle shot hit the walls and windows. Someone had set the kitchen on fire. Men were dismounting and raiding the barns and outbuildings. Warriors were on the porches. John Horse rode past the house to the woods on the other side. He tied his horse and ran back on foot. He liked to touch the land; he could move more stealthily on foot. He ran back toward the house, his heart racing in his chest. This was his first time on raids. It felt odd. He held his rifle in one hand and his ax in the other. He jumped and climbed onto the veranda. He broke the window in the door and cautiously looked in. It was dark inside and he could discern no person. He kicked the door open and entered. It was a woman's room. He took the comb off the dresser and put it in his pouch for his wife. He ran out and jumped to the ground. He ran for the woods as the raid was nearly over. It had been an easy raid because it seemed no one was home. As he ran down the path he heard something. He raised his ax when he encountered someone. It was a white woman with her children clinging to her skirts. She hugged her children closer. He could see she was helpless. She held no weapon and her fists were tiny. He lowered his ax and motioned her to follow. At first she just stood there frozen with fear but when John Horse prompted her to follow a second time, she did. Within the hour John Horse could see the fires from the white army camp.

"Go and be safe. I have a family that is deep in my heart too." He pointed to the camp.

"Thank you. I am Mary Godfrey[2]." She extended her hand to John Horse in a gesture of friendship. "I will not forget this." The woman and her children hurried toward the camp. [2]

When the raid was over, John Horse returned to John Caesar's camp. Most of the enslaved blacks had returned to their plantations. Osceola, who had been waiting at camp during the raid, greeted Cowokoci and John Caesar. They sat in council when John Horse arrived after escorting Mary Godfrey to safety.

"We are expecting a boat from Cuba tomorrow. It will dock in Charleston and our friends the enslaved Africans will unload the boat. They will smuggle the arms we purchased onto a boat and float it down to Florida where we will meet it. We can pick it up just south of Georgia and north of Jacksonville near the Kinglsey plantation. The people who live there are friendly to our cause.

"Thank you John Caesar for all you do," said John Horse. The next day John Horse, Cowokoci, and Osceola obtained the guns and headed back to the tribe. They were very careful not to be seen and traveled long into the night. Their cargo was too precious to risk an encounter with the white soldiers. It represented many Indian lives saved.

Twelve

Things were routine for the next few months. The Indians stockpiled shot and powder getting ready for an inevitable war. In small groups they visited the army forts occasionally giving the appearance of acquiescence. These small groups of Indians obtained supplies and food and agreed with the soldiers that they should leave. The only disagreement was when the great emigration would take place. General Clinch, in charge of the Florida campaign at the time of the treaty, had granted the tribes permission to delay emigration until their pleas were heard in Washington so long as they promised to go eventually. The white soldiers and settlers thought this pacified the Indians for a while. They considered the danger passed and expected to live in peace. Many settlers were waiting in northern Florida and southern Georgia ready to rush in and take over Indian lands as soon as they left. It was a time of apprehensive optimism for the white American community. The raids on the coast disturbed them but the settlers were told that this was a small band of renegade Indians who would soon be captured or killed.

Osceola would visit the fort at times; he could not hide his anger and he was cold to people who had previously been his friends. There was an uneasy peace, but it was peace nonetheless until General Thompson did something that the Seminole Nation considered an outright act of war. He prohibited the sale of powder and shot to any Indian. It was already illegal for any black man to have a gun, shot, or powder. Osceola became very angry when he heard this.

"What is wrong with these people?" he asked of his companions. "Do they not know we need to hunt to feed our families?" Then he approached General Thompson. He was seething with vile. "Am I black? A slave? My skin is dark, but I am an Indian, a Seminole. I will make the white man red with blood and then blacken him in the sun and rain. The animals will smell his bones and the buzzard will eat his flesh."

General Thompson was incensed. He was determined to control Osceola and break his spirit. Doing so would make General Thompson a hero among his peers. He ordered Osceola arrested and confined in irons. Osceola's companions immediately fled the fort and returned to the Indian camp with the news. All fled but his wife, Morning Dew.

Morning Dew was taken. [3]

Osceola's wife, a black woman, was the daughter of an Indian chief and a runaway enslaved African. She was at the edge of camp waiting for Osceola.

When he was arrested, she was stunned and hesitated there a moment when she should have been fleeing the soldier's camp. Slavers snuck up behind her and grabbed her. They quickly spirited her away before Osceola knew what had happened. She fought and kicked and bit but she was small and the slavers were large smelly men. Osceola heard her but he was in chains and could not have prevented it anyway. The slave hunters believed that they had the right to capture runaway slaves and their children. The Indians insisted she was a free woman and a Seminole but the white slave hunters did not care about the Seminole's claims. In fact they cared about very little but the money they would make selling their captured Seminoles.

Emathla was in counsel with Micanopy when the men approached.

"General Thompson has arrested Osceola," they reported.

"And they took his wife."

"This is an outrage," said Emathla. John Horse and Cowokoci approached and overheard the news.

"And he has forbidden Indians from having guns. This made Osceola angry and he threatened General Thompson."

"By their action, the U.S. Government has declared war," stated John Horse.

"This is an outrage," added Cowokoci. "They have no reason so there is no reasoning with them. They have no right to steal free Seminoles be they red or black."

"They will live to regret confining Osceola in irons," said John Horse.

"More so they will regret taking his wife," said Micanopy.

"I will go and see if he can be rescued. If there is a way I will bring him back with me," said Cowokoci. "After we free him, we will see if we can find his wife." He prepared to leave. John Horse followed.

"I am going too," he said and Cowokoci nodded in agreement.

The two friends rode silently each knowing that there was no turning back at this point. The Nation would soon be engaged in a full-scale war. When they neared the fort, they tied-up their horses and approached on foot being careful to remain out of sight. Osceola was shackled and chained in the middle of the Fort. Several soldiers stood guard making communication impossible.

"We have to get him out of there," whispered John Horse.

"I know, but how?" asked Cowokoci. "Attacking the fort would cost Indian lives and someone would probably shoot Osceola at the sound of the war cry."

John Horse whistled like a bird to let Osceola know they were near and appraising the situation. Osceola raised his head and looked in their direction. He nodded acknowledgement. John Horse and Cowokoci headed back to camp. They would report what they found.

Cowokoci approached his father Emathla. "He is in chains and under heavy guard," he said.

"I was afraid of such a thing," Emathla answered.

Micanopy was nearby and walked up and heard Cowokoci. "I think we should appeal to the general," said Micanopy. "I want to delay war as long as possible. The soldiers grow weary of being far from their homes. We grow stronger."

Abraham added, "But when is it long enough? How do we know the best time to engage in war? It is clear they will not go away. More and more come every day."

"Abraham is wise," added John Horse. Every day the white man is nearby is a day of danger that he, Abraham, and their families would be enslaved by the white settlers. John Horse would die first but he did not want this fate for his wife and children, his sister and her children.

"I think we should go and talk," said Micanopy.

"White man's talk is only air. It means nothing," said Emathla. All nodded in agreement. "Let us send a woman and children to take Osceola food and medicine. Let us hear his thoughts."

"Yes, let us do that," said Abraham.

The general did not understand what an insult this was to any Indian but especially to Osceola who was a very proud man. He kept Osceola confined for six days. Every day he asked Osceola if he would emigrate and every day Osceola ignored his presence.

General Thompson finally let him go after the chiefs interceded and convinced General Thompson that Osceola would abide by the treaty. Charlie Emathla personally interceded in convincing General Thompson to let Osceola go.

"He will abide by the treaty," Charlie Emathla pleaded. "If you keep him locked up, it is a bad thing. It is very insulting to such a proud man."

"You say he will agree to emigration?" asked General Thompson.

"Yes, I'm sure he will. He understands your power now and respects it. And if you get his wife back, he will be your ally and friend for life."

General Thompson walked over to Osceola who had been listening to this exchange.

"Is this true?" asked General Thompson. "Are you willing to abide by the treaty?"

"Yes," said Osceola. "I agree and I will bring in my warriors but you must agree to find and return my wife."

"Excellent," boomed Thompson. "I am pleased." He grabbed Osceola's hand and shook it rattling the chains manacled to his wrist. The general laughed and patted him on the back. General Thompson regretted chaining Osceola and the longer it went on, the more he regretted it but he could not just let him go without some kind of assurance of cooperation.

Osceola feigned acquiescence. "We should be friends in peace. No more killing," he said. "What of my wife?"

"I already have men checking on her. I'm sure we will find her and she will come back soon. I sent soldiers after her the minute I heard she was taken. I expect the soldiers to return shortly with your wife."

"Be sure that she returns to me," said Osceola. Osceola was heartbroken over the loss of his lovely young wife. He might have gotten over General Thompson arresting him but he would never forgive Thompson for letting his wife be taken. Morning Dew was a gentle soul. Even if they didn't hurt her, she would be traumatized.

The General was so pleased that Osceola agreed to the treaty that he sent for a prized rifle. He presented it to Osceola.

"This is a token of our friendship. It represents a new beginning."

Osceola took the rifle and thanked the General. In his heart though he knew he would one day shoot General Thompson with this rifle. There was a small chance peace could be attained between the Seminoles and the Americans but with the kidnapping of Osceola's wife that small chance was gone. Many of the chiefs had mixed race children and grandchildren and just like with Morning Dew, the slave hunters felt they had the right to seize them. The chiefs thought they could negotiate and keep their families intact but now they realized that was not true. If they would take from Osceola, they would take from them all. War was the only possibility.

Anyone who opposed war was now an enemy to the Seminole, even if that person was Seminole.

Thirteen

There was much talk among the Seminoles as to emigration. Most opposed it but a few were willing to go to avoid war. Charlie Emathla was one of them. Osceola warned all Indians that if a man agreed to emigration, that man was his enemy. Charlie Emathla argued with Osceola.

"I am tired. I do not want to fight. I can live happily in the west. It would save many lives to just go. I am old. I want to enjoy my family in peace."

Incensed, Osceola replied, "I'm telling you now Charlie Emathla, if you take one step toward surrender I will see that you never make it to the west."

"Osceola, why are you so angry with me? Did I not secure your release from the fort?"

"Yes, and I thank you for that but if our people splinter into groups, we will not survive. You should have let me die in that cage if you intend to go west."

"This is not productive," said Abraham trying to diffuse the situation. "We must stick together. To fight among ourselves is exactly what the white soldiers want."

"Calm down Osceola," interjected Micanopy. "Abraham is right. We may disagree but we are united in our heritage and struggle."

"I will not calm down. If we do not stay united with one vision, we will perish in this land. For me I will die here be it now by the white man or later as an old man called by the Creator but I will die here on my lands."

Charlie Emathla shaking his head walked away. He called his family and followers and led them from camp.

"He is a weak link," said Osceola.

"No he is not; he is a Seminole," said Micanopy.

Osceola stared at Micanopy. His icy stare was penetrating and it unnerved Micanopy. Micanopy looked away but continued talking.

"Osceola, you are a good man. You are a great warrior but you are not a chief. These decisions rest with the chiefs."

It was true. Osceola had no hereditary right be chief. He was becoming a strong force in the tribe though. He earned his status on the battlefield. Many warriors followed him and listened to his council. John Horse and Cowokoci were both emerging as leaders of their clans. They respected and followed Osceola. Micanopy was the chief but he was old and weak. The tribe knows he listens to Abraham who has much influence in the tribe's affairs. Fortunately Abraham was a good man with the tribe's welfare at heart. But Osceola was quickly becoming the War Chief. He was the war spirit.

"I understand Osceola's position," said John Horse. "In war, the weakest must be sacrificed."

"The women and children are the weakest," said Micanopy.

"But they must be protected," said John Horse. "They are not men."

"I don't like where this is going," said Abraham. "I will follow my chief Micanopy but I am frightened for my people and their families. There are more and more raids by slave hunters. They do not care that we are free black men. They do not care that we are Seminole. If the soldiers could guarantee freedom, I would listen to what they have to say, but they cannot guarantee anything. One white leader does not know what the other white leader is saying and doing. One promises and another breaks the promise. We cannot believe anything they say especially their guarantees that we would be safe in the west. We would not be safe among Creeks. The Creeks are our enemies. They betrayed us by fighting against us with the white soldiers. They have taken our people into chattel slavery."

All nodded their heads in agreement. Cowokoci and Emathla had remained quiet during the heated words of Osceola and Charlie Emathla. Emathla was passive and did not desire to fight any more than Charlie Emathla did, but his sons, especially Cowokoci, were cold warriors. Cowokoci did what needed to be done to protect and preserve his people and their heritage; he would abide by Osceola's decision regarding Charlie Emathla. Emathla knew this. He also knew he would have to choose a side very soon. He was leaning toward Osceola because he preferred to remain allied with strength, with his sons. He preferred to remain loyal to family.

Fourteen

The Tribe spent the next few months preparing for war. John Horse spent most of his time recruiting the plantation slaves from the east coast and meeting with the fisherman from Cuba and the Bahamas to trade for arms. These activities were especially crucial at this point because General Thompson had banned the sale of arms and ammunition to the Seminoles and yet he had given Osceola a rifle. This did not make sense to the Seminoles. They cannot take the soldier's words seriously when they say one thing and do another.

While the tribe prepared for war, Charlie Emathla prepared for emigration.

Osceola was incensed. He confronted Charlie Emathla when he was returning from selling his cattle. His people were following him.

"Charlie Emathla, what do you think you are doing?" asked Osceola. As he spoke Osceola's followers surrounded Charlie Emathla on all sides.

"I am protecting my family. I am leaving before war can begin."

"You are a coward," said Osceola in a cold low tone. His voice sounded like the growl of the wild panther. His eyes shot sparks of anger.

"I am not a coward. I am a man who understands the futility of fighting the wave of white immigration into Florida. We cannot fight it. It will not stop. It will continue long after you and I have gone to the Creator. I am old. I only wish for peace."

"We can and we will defeat them," stated Osceola in the same cold tone. "A man fights for his family. A coward runs."

"Osceola, be reasonable," he pleaded.

"This is reason," he said and he aimed his rifle at Charlie Emathla who looked to Osceola with eyes wide and mouth open. Before he could plead for his life, Osceola shot him dead. To John Horse it seemed as if he fell in slow motion, as if his brain did not comprehend what his body knew; he was done. His family and followers scattered. Osceola picked up the bag of gold coins Charlie Emathla had been holding from selling his cattle. He emptied them into his hand and scattered them to the winds.

"No one touch this tainted gold. It is made from the red man's blood. No one touch this coward's body. It is food for the buzzards."

Charlie Emathla's gold and remains lay untouched for two years, because no white man went there, and no Indian respecting Osceola's decree would touch it.

This was the first act of the Second Seminole War. It frightened the white settlers. If he would kill his own, what would he do to his enemy? There was talk of Osceola's aggression in every corner of society. It even reached mainstream northern newspapers. The populous, especially those in the north of the United States, was not in favor of war with the Seminoles. Most people saw no reason to expend life and fortune to win a piece of swamp which is what they thought of Florida at the time. To increase the anxiety, Emathla joined John Caesar in stepping up the raids east of the St. John's River near St. Augustine. In just two days they sacked and looted five plantations. Great numbers of enslaved Africans fled their bondage sparking the largest slave revolt in the continental United States.

"Look John Caesar, I have painted my face red," said one African who had just joined John Caesar's tribe.

"Yes I see that," replied John Caesar.

"I am now Seminole. I am symbolizing my allegiance to the red man with my red face. I am no longer slave to the white man. I am free!" They laughed and others took up the war paint and painted their faces too.

This was very upsetting to the white Americans in the southern states. They feared a full-scale slave rebellion which is exactly what they had in Florida. Such an act would leave the south financially devastated and many of the plantation owners dead. These factions urged President Jackson to escalate the war, something President Jackson was eager to do.

John Horse knew many of these fleeing slaves because of his activities on the coast. He welcomed them into his tribe. Abraham was very pleased with John Horse as he watched the people from the plantations arrive and join the tribe.

"You have done well John Horse," he said one day.

"Thank you Abraham. These men are good warriors. I rode with many of them on John Caesar's raids."

"This is good. John Horse, you are a man of importance in the tribe. You take your duty seriously."

John Horse swelled with pride. "Thank you for your faith in me."

"You will be called on for very serious duty in the coming months. War is a very difficult time for all."

"Do you think we can win?" asked John Horse.

"Yes. I do. I know we must win or our families will be scattered throughout the lands. We will never reunite if that happens. It is very sad to lose a family member to slavery. Never knowing where they are or if they are alive is a very hard thing to endure."

John Horse nodded. By nature John Horse was not a violent person. He did not take pleasure in defeating the enemy as Osceola and Cowokoci did. He only fought for his family's freedom. It was his duty and he took it seriously. John Horse also felt the Seminole could win. He has watched the white soldiers and they are not suited for fighting in Florida. They wear heavy wool clothing which overheats their bodies and makes them weak. They fight in lines. They march in the hot afternoon sun. They listen to their leader's orders before acting. Seminoles fight individually. They know what to do and in one large cohesive group they do what is needed individually. If a warrior is lost, the others continue. If an Army officer is lost, the men flounder running in circles unsure of what to do next.

The chiefs are very smart. *The white soldiers do not give us credit for intelligence*, he thought. *They think the Indians are childish. Even Brooks called the tribesmen children. This is why we will win. We will outsmart them. We will outlast them.* Seminoles were smart fighters. They never engaged in a fight in which they could not escape. They fled the talks because the soldiers had many guns aimed at them. To fight then, would have been suicide. The Seminoles manipulated battles to take place where they had the advantage. If the soldiers outnumbered them, they faded into the swamps. The soldiers were ill equipped to follow, and the Indians easily escaped. If the Indians had the advantage, they would not flee into the swamps; they fought, they were superior in battle and easily defeated their enemies.

This is exactly what happened to Major Dade.

Fifteen

The Seminoles planned an attack. The chiefs and warriors sat in council.

"We understand that the soldiers will be marching from Fort Brooke to Fort King. Our friend, Louis Pacheco, has informed us," said Micanopy. "He is a slave on loan to the army as an interpreter."

"This is good to know," said Cowokoci.

"Thank you John Horse for slipping into the white community as a spy and keeping us informed of the soldiers' movements," said Micanopy.

John Horse nodded. He was proud to be of service. It was dangerous work because many of the soldiers knew him from his past dealings at Fort Brooke when he sold gopher turtles and ran errands for the soldiers. However he was a man now and known for his kempt style. He made himself sloppy; he didn't bathe and the soldiers never recognized him. John Horse had always enjoyed duping the white man. Most of them acted superior to the blacks and Indians and the Indians were smart enough to use this attitude to their advantage.

"The troops should be well-supplied," added Emathla. I assume they are to take provisions to Fort King.

"Yes. That is why I think we should attack. Let us keep the soldiers on the defensive," added Abraham. "And at the same time, we will acquire shot, powder, and food from the soldiers."

"I don't know," said Ote Emathla. "The longer we wait, the wearier the soldiers become." Ote Emathla was not sure about starting a war but he was hesitant to express his doubts in front of Osceola, especially after the death of Charlie Emathla. Ote Emathla was a chief by heredity; he had a right to his opinion. However, Osceola was the warrior who embodied the spirit of Seminole freedom. He was honored as a chief because of his deeds. He was a great war chief.

"They are weary already," said Osceola. "It is time to act. It is time to show the great white father that we are not his children."

"True," said Cowokoci. "And if we take their supplies, they will be short of food which will contribute to their weakness."

John Horse spoke. "It is right to attack this army. The supplies that are needed at Fort King will not reach there; therefore we hit them twice with one fight."

The warriors mumbled among themselves. John Horse was right of course. They could not argue that point, besides most agreed with Osceola anyway. They knew it was time to take charge of this war but most and John Horse were not looking forward to it. The Seminole had been preparing for this for over a year. It was time. They planned a double attack.

"Then it is settled," said Micanopy. "We will attack the soldiers when they are marching and when it is to our advantage."

"I would like to attack General Thompson first," interjected Osceola.

"I think we can work that out," said Emathla. "It would be much easier after the majority of the soldiers leave the army fort. Then you can join the rest of the tribe in attacking the soldiers."

"That would work," said Abraham. "It would also send a message that we mean business. It will appear that we are everywhere at once."

"Once we do this, there will be no turning back," said Cowokoci.

"I know but I don't know what else we can do," said Micanopy. "We have tried to live in peace with the white settlers. They just don't want it. Even when they are pretending to be our friends, they allow slave hunters to raid our camps stealing our people. I think the time of turning back is already passed." Micanopy was echoing Abraham's advice to him. Abraham was not looking forward to war but he was ready.

"I agree there is no reason to leave our land just because they want to live here without us," said Ote Emathla. "I just think maybe we should try to renegotiate the treaty."

The chiefs began to talk at once.

"We have already tried."

"Who is this President Jackson to order us to move from the land given to us by the Creator?"

"There is no reason in the white man."

"True, true," they all responded in unison.

"We should send Indians to help the white soldiers find their way across the Withlacoochee. That way they will cross where we want them too," said Abraham.

"This is a good tactic," said Micanopy. "Osceola, you take your warriors and deal with General Thompson when he walks after dinner. He is so secure in his mind that he does not fear us. He thinks we are no threat. He thinks he subdued you by putting you in chains. It was a disgrace and he will pay for it now. In the meantime the main force of the Seminoles will sit and wait for the soldiers and ambush them as well."

"I agree with this plan," said Osceola.

"You come as soon as you are done with Thompson," ordered Micanopy. "We will await your arrival before we attack."

"This is a good plan," said John Horse. "We should leave in two days to be ready for the soldiers."

"Then in two days it is," said Osceola. "Let us prepare."

"Yes," said Micanopy. "Let us prepare."

"Once we start, we cannot let up until our victory is declared," said Osceola. "No more talks."

"No more talks." The chiefs agreed.

The Indians broke council and returned to their camps to prepare.

In the meantime, the soldiers were preparing to march from Fort Brooke to Fort King. They weren't especially concerned about the march. After General Thompson locked up Osceola, the consensus was that the Indians had lost their muster, that Osceola was tamed, and the rest would follow him.

This very thinking doomed the soldiers, and their arrogance kept them from realizing it.

Sixteen

"Sir," said Lieutenant Harris, "I estimate the entire Seminole population including both blacks and reds does not exceed three thousand." Lieutenant Harris was the Disbursing Agent for the army command. He was in charge of all the supplies for the army. His job included estimating how long the supplies would last and if rationing was necessary.

"Is this based on good intelligence?" asked General Thompson.

"I do believe so sir. I went over the figures myself. In fact, I think half that number is women and children."

"If this is correct, we should tie up this Florida mess soon," said General Thompson. He was feeling optimistic since he believed he had neutralized Osceola. He had no inkling that Osceola was outside the fort plotting his demise at that very moment.

"Yes sir, I think there are four or five hundred warriors at most."

"Some second-guessed my decision to arrest Osceola but I think in the long run my decision will be seen as correct."

"Yes sir."

"Osceola was out of control and he needed humbling. A week in chains accomplished that."

"Yes sir."

"I think we might have turned the tide on the Indian problem in Florida. I understand that since Osceola killed Charlie Emathla over four hundred Seminoles turned themselves into Fort King for protection."

"That is good news, sir. Of course, the problem of feeding them is an issue."

"Yes but at this rate, we'll have most of them ready to emigrate very soon."

And that is what they believed.

Lieutenant Harris continued figuring how many rations would be needed for the soldiers and the surrendered Seminoles. The men left Fort Brooke with little thought of the Seminoles. It was a chilly morning and the soldiers shivered.

"Oof," said one soldier. "It is cold this morning. I thought Florida was supposed to be tropical."

"I guess it gets cold in the tropics," said another. "What do we know? Ever been in the tropics before?"

"No," chimed in another soldier. "Why do we want this land? Someone remind me."

"I don't know," said another. "Something about taking over the land from sea to sea. Makes no sense to me."

"It's 'cause all those rich folks in the South keep losing their slaves to Florida. That's what it's all about."

"No," said another. "I think it's about the United States wanting to control the whole continent."

"I guess that makes us safer. But if they want the Indians to move to Arkansas, aren't they still on the continent?"

The men puzzled and pondered that thought a moment. As they marched their boots sank into the sandy soil. It made the going rough and slow. When they weren't sinking in sand, swampy water seeped into their boots. Most of the men had their overcoats buttoned, unwisely covering their muskets and powder bags. There was little concern about having a gun ready to fire.

Osceola and his warriors were hiding in the scrub. He was beneath a cabbage palm covered with kudzu vines and he noted the buttoned coats as he watched two lines of soldiers march from the fort. He shook his head and thought this is almost too easy. He nudged John Horse and pointed. John Horse looked at the buttoned coats and shook his head and chuckled. *If the entire tribe was here now, we could take the fort*, he thought. *We could shoot them all before they could even react. Not that it mattered. They would all be dead in a couple of days anyway. They didn't know it, but they were dead men walking.*

After the soldiers passed and the gates to the fort were closed, Osceola signaled for two young braves to come to him.

"You two track behind the soldiers. When the soldiers are within a day's march of the Withlacoochee, one of you ride and tell Micanopy."

The boys nodded.

"If the soldiers do anything I or Micanopy should know about ride and inform us promptly." The boys crept quietly to where the horses were tied. They silently made their way through the scrub keeping a quarter of a mile behind and to the west of the soldiers. They were close enough to hear them but far enough away to remain hidden. Whenever the soldiers stopped, the boys tied the horses and sneaked up close enough to see what the soldiers were doing. Usually they were chatting and eating. They stopped every few hours to rest. Most of the talk was conjecture.

"I think we'll wrap this up pretty soon," said one soldier.

"I hope so. If I had known what this land was all about, I don't think I would have joined," said another.

"Amen, brother," added another. "I just want to get home to my family. This soldierin' ain't what it's cracked up to be."

The men chatted aimlessly complaining about the conditions. This one's back ached. Another's foot was swollen. Several could not take the insects a moment longer. Another was cold and couldn't get warm, and they all dreamed of being home.

Seventeen

Meanwhile Osceola and his sixty warriors lie in wait outside the fort. They waited patiently for two days. General Thompson did not leave the fort on the first day but on the second day he did. He was having a cordial dinner with his lieutenants. "The weather is pleasantly warm this evening," he said.

"I guess the chill has passed," said one lieutenant. "The weather in Florida is fickle. One day's hot, the next day's cold. One minute it's sunny and the next minute we're being drenched in a torrential downpour."

"Isn't that the truth?" said Lieutenant Smith. "Sometimes we're in a torrential downpour with the sun shining." The men all laughed.

"Smith," said General Thompson. "I think I'll take a stroll after dinner. I'd like you to join me. I want to discuss something."

"Certainly sir," said Lieutenant Smith. "I think it's pretty safe. The Indians haven't been around in a while. I guess they are deep in the swamps hiding from us.

"We have them on the run for sure. Let me grab a couple of cigars from my desk and we'll go."

The general and the lieutenant casually strolled from the fort. "I've been cooped up in my quarters doing paperwork all day. I'd like a little fresh air and exercise."

"The air is certainly clear and crisp this evening. I can see why people love this place. You don't get winter evenings like this in Kentucky."

"No you don't," agreed General Thompson. He lit two cigars and handed one to Lieutenant Smith.

"Thank you sir," he said. "While I admit it is a little chilly, the setting sun is warm."

"I'm not sure how to interpret the death of Charlie Emathla. Was Osceola acting as a hostile chief to send a message to the other chiefs or was he acting under the direction of the other chiefs?"

"I don't know General," said Lieutenant Smith. "I guess we need to figure it out though to know what our next course of action should be. Have we asked the Seminoles that come for rations?"

General Thompson shook his head. "Yes, but very few come in these days. Most of the time they talk in circles. The information they impart is of little use."

"It is possible that his execution had nothing to do with emigration. It could have been a personal problem between Osceola and Charlie Emathla."

"True but Charlie Emathla did negotiate for Osceola's release when he was under arrest."

"It is a mystery, sir."

The general and the lieutenant strolled and the Indians concealed in the scrub watched. They lie within thirty feet of the road. Thompson and Smith suspected nothing.

Many of Osceola's followers were black men who had escaped enslavement during the attacks on the east coast plantations. They had happily joined the rebellion for a chance at a free life in the interior of Florida. Many burned their plantation homes as they left. It was these men who, with the Black Seminoles, would fight to the death. Their lives and freedom depended on it. Osceola knew this and took charge of this group of warriors. He knew these men would be the most savage fighters. The red Seminoles were determined to stay on their lands and to move west would be a hardship but their families would remain intact. The black men would be made into slaves and lose their families.

Osceola watched. He waited for General Thompson to walk a good distance from the fort. He wanted the general to feel secure and safe on his walk. He continued to watch as the general and Smith walked towards Erasmus Roger's trading post. When the they were about three hundred yards from the fort and on the crest of a hill visible from the fort, Osceola stood up, caught the general's eye, stared intently with all the hate and vengeance in his soul, screamed his bone-chilling war whoop, aimed the rifle that was a gift from General Thompson and fired a shot that hit Thompson square in the chest. Sixty rifles followed suit. General Thompson and Lieutenant Smith were killed instantly. Osceola ran from the scrub and stabbed the dead General Thompson in the heart. He scalped him and cut the scalp into many pieces so each man could have a trophy. He tied a piece of the scalp to his belt and felt the general's warm blood drip down his leg.

"Mock me. Lock me in irons," he said to the corpse. "What do you have to say now to your red children?"

The sentry on duty in the fort witnessed the brutality and was frozen in horror. The celebratory yells unnerved the rest of soldiers in the fort.

"Shut the gates!" yelled a sentry coming to his senses. "They've killed General Thompson!"

Panic ran through the soldiers that were left in the fort. There was only one company of forty-six men and they assumed the full force of the Seminole Nation was at the gate. They prepared to defend, but mostly they cowered inside.

At the trading post, Erasmus Rogers and his clerks were having dinner. They attempted to flee to the fort for safety when they heard the gunshots but the Indians overtook them and they were killed just outside the fort. Osceola and the men looted the trading post taking the supplies that would benefit the tribe and the war effort. Osceola also took for a trophy a blue army coat. They set fire to the buildings as they rode away. They would soon meet up with Micanopy and the tribe at the Withlacoochee.

Eighteen

The soldiers that had left Fort Brook five days earlier were hungry and tired and cold. Their overcoats were still buttoned over their cartridge boxes. They knew nothing of Osceola's revenge so they were somewhat complacent. Louis Pacheco, a slave on loan as a guide, was at the head of the march. Eight officers and one hundred and two soldiers followed this lowly slave. He rode next to Major Dade and he was leading the soldiers directly into an ambush, even if he wasn't sure of it himself until he heard the war cry.

Major Dade has been very careful in picking the night camp sites. He was wary of an attack. However for five days he had seen no sign of any hostiles and he was beginning to relax. All the while, the Seminoles had been tracking the soldiers waiting for the perfect opportunity for attack.

"The pine thicket at Wahoo swamp will be the best place to attack," said Emathla.

"It is a good spot," said Halpatter Tustenugee. "But we are to wait for Osceola and Micanopy."

"Micanopy will be here very soon. As to Osceola, I assume he is close but I do not know."

"This is the best place. The soldiers are too far from either fort to expect reinforcements."

"This is true," added a warrior. "We should attack when it is to our advantage. To wait for Osceola might lesson our advantage."

"That's true," said Halpatter Tustenugee.

Micanopy arrived as they were talking.

"What is the situation?" he asked.

"We are thinking the pine thicket at Wahoo swamp is the best place to attack," said Emathla. "The soldiers have crossed the Withlacoochee and are feeling secure. They have relaxed their guard a little."

"Is Osceola nearby?" asked Micanopy.

"This we do not know," said Tustenugee, "but with one hundred and eighty warriors here, it is of little matter."

"We promised to wait," protested Micanopy. Was Micanopy stalling or was he concerned with Osceola's reaction if he changed the plan to wait?

"I know," said Tustenugee, "but the soldiers will be sitting ducks at this juncture. If we wait, we will lesson our advantage. If the battle goes against us, we can retreat into the Wahoo Swamp where the soldiers cannot follow efficiently."

"Okay then," said Micanopy. "We will attack in the morning when they least expect it." *After all*, he thought, *I am chief. I can make this decision and Osceola will have to understand.*

"Morning is best," added Halpatter Tustenugee. "The soldiers are cold and they button their coats over their shot and powder. This is not very smart. We will hit them before they can react."

Micanopy agreed but he was nervous. He was an old man and with his advisor Abraham off with Osceola, he was apprehensive but he understood that his age made him fear. He knew this war must take place. He knew the white man could not be trusted. They continued to take free Seminoles into slavery regardless of talks and promises. They did not respect the Indians. They wanted them to change and live as the white man does. This was not the Indian way.

So on the morning of December twenty-eighth, in the year eighteen thirty-five, the Seminoles concealed in the pine thicket awaited the soldiers approach. Some were in the trees with Spanish moss stuck to them with mud. This served as an excellent camouflage because the warriors blended in with the trees. Besides most of the soldiers looked down as they walked to watch for tripping hazards and deadly snakes like rattlers and cottonmouth in the pathway. It was clear from their demeanor that marching in Florida was hard and most regretted being here. Sometimes entire companies passed under the noses of Seminole scouts and not one of them ever looked up, not one of them ever suspected.

Suddenly a gray horse appeared on the trail in front of the soldiers. Major Dade noticed it. He looked to Louis Pacheco for a possible explanation but before he could ask, he heard Halpatter Tustenugee's war whoop and was cut down. Micanopy carried to the battle by young braves, his advanced age apparent, fired the first shot hitting Major Dade in the chest and killing him immediately. Louis Pacheco fell to the ground feigning death and was "captured" by the Seminoles. He spent the remainder of the war fighting on the side of the Indians. Years later he claimed he did not knowingly lead the army into the ambush but that has always been suspect. Upon hearing the first shot, the Seminoles' war whoops reverberated through the ranks of the soldiers and they shuddered. Panic ran through the ranks as their fellow soldiers fell dead all around. The first volley from the concealed Indians had cut down half the company.

"Quickly men, prepare to fire," yelled one officer. "Cover the artillery. Get the cannon ready." The survivors of the first attack quickly jumped behind trees and fired back at the Seminoles.

"Fire," yelled an artillery man. The six-pound cannon boomed loudly as the ball flew at the Seminoles. It exploded in the trees and debris rained down on the warriors. The balls flew over the Seminoles' heads and as soon as the smoke cleared, Seminoles killed the artillery men. The soldiers that survived the first attack had used the cannon fire for cover, and then they mounted a breastwork defense. They quickly felled trees, stacking the logs three high and hid behind them for cover. The Seminoles continued to approach often enough to force the soldiers to continue the assault. By noon, the artillery was spent. With the threat of the cannon neutralized, the Seminoles advanced and fired so many shots at the breastwork that the remaining soldiers were killed where they crouched, their guns still aimed at the Indians. Halpatter Tustenugee, Ote Emathla, and several warriors entered the log pen. A man was alive. He snatched a rifle from one warrior and hit him so hard in the head that he killed the brave, his brains bashed out of his head. The soldier ran down the path; two warriors on horses overtook him and shot him dead. He fell face down in the mud joining his comrades. Bodies and blood were everywhere. Even the oxen that pulled the canon laid dead.

Osceola and his warriors arrived near the end of the battle and black warriors previously escaped from enslavement rode through the camp with axes killing any soldier that showed signs of life. They looted and mutilated the bodies spurred on by their anger from previous enslavement. When they had finished, there was not a sign of life from the soldiers.

The Indians gathered in the swamp to assess the battle. Three warriors were killed, five wounded, and over a hundred soldiers lay dead.

"You didn't wait for me," said Osceola. He was wearing the blue U.S. Army jacket that he had taken during his attack on General Thompson.

"We did not know where you were and this was the perfect spot for battle. The swamp provided an escape route and the soldiers were sitting ducks."

"You did very well today Micanopy," said Osceola. "The great white father should soon realize we are not his children," his hatred of the white men was apparent in his voice. "This bloody battlefield is retaliation for the offenses of my childhood. The soldiers killed many brethren and burned many Indian homes when Andrew Jackson marched into my village. I was a child but I remember the fear in my mother's eyes as we escaped south."

"I have the same memories," said John Horse. "This is a great victory."

"True," said Cowokoci. "We have tried to live in peace. This is the only solution. We should not let down our guard until all the soldiers are dead or gone from our lands."

The warriors nodded in agreement. The victory was uplifting and the Indians celebrated. Micanopy was relieved that Osceola approved of his decision to fight without him. Osceola contributed the spoils from trading post and the warriors whooped and hollered long into the night. One brave mounted Wiley Thompson's scalp on a pole and danced around it.

"Now my red children, you must do what is best for the country," he mocked imitating the speeches he had heard often from General Thompson. The Indians laughed and joined in.

"The Great White Father cares for his red children," said another as he fell on the ground laughing. The Seminoles were enjoying the victory. They had prepared for this moment for an entire year. They deserved their revenge and their celebration.

John Horse watched from outside the circle. He sat in the dark watching the glowing fires and he thought *the war is begun; there is no turning back now.* He had prepared his entire life for this moment. His fate was sealed the day he ran from Payne's Prairie as a little boy carrying eggs and escaping Jackson's invading army.

Eggs, what a silly thing, he thought and it made him chuckle. He was born in a time of turmoil and all his days on this earth would be dominated by war and the search for freedom.

Nineteen

The next morning, the Indians awoke slowly; their party had lasted long into the night. Osceola sat by the fire. Econchattemicco, called the Red Ground King, joined him. He was a chief well known to Osceola.

"I have not expressed my sadness for you in losing your wife."

"Thank you Econchattemicco. It is very sad. I understand you too are sad."

"Yes, it is true. My granddaughter was taken, and we have been unable to determine her whereabouts. My children are very distraught. She is my joy and my joy is gone."

"This is why we can never compromise. The white man lies and cheats the red man and then look us in the face and say friend. Slavery is a vile situation. A man who cannot do his work without enslaving people is not a man."

"Yes, slavery is very bad. I see the white people with their children. They seem to hold them and kiss them but if they feel as we do, how could they steal another's child?"

"I do not know. I have wondered that myself. My father is a white man and he did move away and leave us. I thank the Creator that he left me with my mother, a Red-Stick Creek. I am Creek. I am Miccosukee. I am Seminole. I am not white. I abhor the white ways. I do not think the white people have feelings or how could my father have walked away from me and never see me again?"

As they were talking John Horse and Cowokoci awoke and were sharing some coonti bread. Young braves scouting the area rode into camp.

"The enemy is near," they shouted. The chiefs and warriors gathered to hear. "General Clinch is marching nearby. He has probably seven hundred soldiers. He is looking for us."

"Let us make another decisive blow against the soldiers," said Cowokoci. "That will send a message to Washington."

"Yes," agreed Micanopy. "I guess the time for talks has passed." Micanopy usually reluctant to fight was now ready. "Tell the Indian guides to lead the soldiers to the bend in the river. We will leave a canoe so they can cross. When they cross, we will open fire." Micanopy even in his advanced age had lucid thoughts once in a while.

"This is a good plan," said Osceola. "I want to hit them again and again."

The guides nodded and rode out to communicate with the Indians guiding the soldiers.

Major General Clinch had been searching for the Seminoles. He left Fort Brooks with his command and ten days rations. He expected to find and eradicate the Indians quickly. He had seventy friendly Indians guiding him. However the friendly Indians were consuming supplies and leading him in circles.

"Where is the crossing?" General Clinch demanded of the Indian guides.

The Indian who seemed to be the leader turned to talk to the others. They all talked at once, each pointing a different direction. The General was becoming impatient with their talk. He could not understand what they were saying.

"We are not sure," said the Indian guide. "The river is swollen and we do not recognize the spot. The water has covered the crossing."

General Clinch was frustrated. He knew he had few supplies left and he would have to return to the fort soon. "There have been too many missed opportunities with these Indians," he thought. He had naively expected to do what others could not.

"Let us try this way. I'm sure it is this way," said the guide.

"It had better be there," said General Clinch. He ordered the soldiers to march. This they did. Soon they came upon a canoe tied to a tree on the bank of the river.

"This is the spot," insisted the guide. "I know it is. This is why we leave the canoe so others can find it."

"Finally," said the General. He commanded the regular army soldiers to cross in the canoe. Seven men at a time crossed. When the two-hundred and fifty regulars had crossed, Osceola stepped from the scrub. He was a stark figure in the blue U.S. Army coat he had taken from Fort King, his black hair shining blue in the morning sun. The sight of him unnerved many of the soldiers. The blue coat told the soldiers that some of theirs had died at his hands and many more were about to. He held his rifle in the air and started the fray with his war cry.

"Whoooop, whoop, whoooop," he yelled. The full force of the Seminoles opened fire on the army. Panic ran through the ranks. Osceola's war cry always had that effect. The blue U.S. Army jacket was a subtle message that he could take what he wanted whenever he wanted. And right now he wanted them dead. The volunteers left on the other side of the river were of little help. Lieutenant Gains tried to mount a defense but again the army was a sitting duck. The volunteers refused to attempt to cross the river under fire and join the regulars in what was clearly a losing battle. The volunteers' tour of duty was up the next day and they did not wish to die this close to going home. The regular soldiers struggled to get back across the river and General Clinch was forced to retreat. Out of rations and with scores of his company wounded, he retreated to his own plantation which he renamed Fort Drane. The next day, he received a letter from Osceola.

You have guns and so have we, you have powder and lead, and so have we, your men will fight, and so will ours, till the last drop of the white man's blood has moistened the dust of this hunting ground.

Clinch held the letter. He was unnerved but did not show it to his men. This war was proving difficult. He was beginning to doubt his ability to conquer the Seminoles and this god-forsaken land called Florida.

Twenty

The war was not going well for the U.S. Army despite the fact that Washington was pouring unprecedented sums of money into the effort. The plantation owners from the east coast of Florida were crowded into St. Augustine afraid to be caught outside the protection of the city. From behind the city walls they watched the smoke from their burning plantations rise to the heavens. This unnerved them and the citizenry complained bitterly. General Scott was sent by Washington to oversee the army in Florida. President Jackson was frustrated with his generals. Nothing had gone well and maybe Scott could turn the Florida situation around. At least he hoped so because he was running out of generals to send.

Much to President Jackson's chagrin, nothing went right for Scott either. His first problems involved communication. He pleaded with Washington for reinforcements. He informed President Jackson that there was a strong relationship between the Black Seminoles and the plantation slaves. As soon as the war began nearly four hundred slaves defected to the Seminoles. He admitted that this plan had obviously been in the works for some time. He wondered what else the Seminoles might be planning. There was much doubt in the wisdom of continuing this conflict. Seminoles were a remote concept to the citizens in the north. It was a very unpopular war. The volunteers were on the east coast attempting to protect the plantations that were still standing. Washington's response to all arguments and pleading to stop the war was to keep on fighting. President Jackson's goal was to conquer Florida at all costs. He had hoped to sell homesteads in Florida to offset the ever-growing debt from this war. To stop would be to admit defeat. Something Jackson would never do. He had a deep-seated hate for Indians. He lost a brother at the hands of Indians, and his hate had not lessened from the time he had conquered the Creeks in Alabama and Georgia and moved his command south into Spanish Florida virtually invading a foreign land. These events made him a national hero, and that momentum carried him all the way to the White House. He would never give up now.

A volunteer fanned away mosquitoes occasionally smacking himself to kill a biting insect. The bellow of an alligator unnerved the camp. "I didn't know what I was signing up for," he said.

"I know. Why anyone wants this god-forsaken swamp is beyond me," said his companion. "Listen to that. What was that?" he said, his voice rose with his fear.

"I think it's one of those gators. I hear they can run on land faster than a man. Scary."

"I'll say. The only perfect paradise I see here is for Indians and alligators."

"I just want to go home. I have no interest in killing Indians." His companion nodded in agreement. He swatted at insects, a constant activity for the soldiers.

In the meantime, General Edmund P. Gaines, a former Tennessee lawyer who had served in the War of 1812, not realizing that President Jackson had sent General Scott to command Florida, left New Orleans with his troops. He assumed he would receive the assignment and wanted to waste no time in taking command of Florida. He was another man who was sure he could do what others could not. He landed in Tampa and proceeded to the Withlacoochee River to engage the Seminoles.

On the march he came across the bodies of the soldiers killed in Major Dade's battle. The soldiers in the front slowed as they took in the scene.

"Oh my God," one soldier said as he looked around at the skeletal remains of an army. Most just stared in wide-eyed astonishment. A hush fell over the troops as they slowly realized what they had come upon. One soldier dropped to his knees and prayed for the deposed. Several others joined him. Two dead oxen blocked the road, their yokes still around their necks as if they had just lain down to sleep. The decayed bodies of Dade's command were strewn about the ground. Most had been shot in the head and neck. The flies were insufferable. They buzzed biting the men as they stood in awe of the scene in front of them. It was apparent that Major Dade had put up a fight that lasted for some time. A triangular breastwork hastily constructed during the fight was in the middle of the battleground. Some thirty bodies behind it, killed where they lay defending themselves against the Seminoles, their guns still aimed toward the aggressors and ready. To the soldiers it seemed as a moment frozen in time. The horror of the battle lingered on the wind. The soldiers could imagine hearing the screams and cries of the dying men.

"These men must be buried in a proper Christian ceremony," commanded General Gaines. "But first they must all be identified and accounted for."

The soldiers went about the task in a somber mood. Most of the dead were well known to the men in Gaines's command. After the men were buried, several men fished the six-pound cannon from the swamp where the Indians had tossed it. They placed it at the head of the graves to serve as a marker and memorial. General Gaines spoke to Captain Hitchcock.

"This is a very unnerving scene Hitchcock."

"Yes sir it is."

"I'm concerned that I have not heard from General Clinch."

"It is a concern sir," Captain Hitchcock looked around. An eerie feeling came over him. "You don't think he too has met this same fate? Are they watching us now? Planning?" He visibly shuddered at the thought.

"I hope not. I think we will continue to Fort King. To return to Fort Brooke where there are no supplies anyway might appear as a sign of weakness. I don't think we can show any weakness to the enemy at this juncture."

"Yes sir, but Fort King is fifty miles away. We will be vulnerable the entire distance."

"Yes we will have to keep up our guard."

The eerie feeling that Captain Hitchcock was feeling was not without merit. Seminole scouts were watching the soldiers' every move. They were concealed in the scrub and in the trees. The army as usual was unaware of their presence.

Twenty-one

Seminole Scouts rode into camp to report General Gaines's movements. Osceola met them.

"He's got about a thousand men. Right now they are burying the soldiers killed east of Wahoo Swamp two moons ago," said one scout.

Osceola shook his head. "We will let them finish this task. To prevent these actions might be bad medicine. Let us talk."

The leaders of the rebellion under the leadership of Osceola sat in a circle to discuss the next move.

Halpatter Tustenugee spoke first. "It appears that this General Gaines is on his way to Fort King."

"Fort King has no supplies," said Ote Emathla. "This we know."

Cowokoci laughed. "We know more about the white man's army than they do."

All laughed and shook their heads in agreement with Cowokoci.

"We must plan our next move carefully," said Abraham. "Another decisive victory will certainly send a message to the white father in Washington."

"Will it?" asked John Horse. "Is Washington capable of hearing a message? Our spies tell us that General Clinch is begging the white father to quit this war and leave us to our land, but he is stubborn and will not listen to the counsel of his own chiefs."

"That is why we will not send such a victory message," said Osceola. "We will leave no one alive to deliver any message."

Osceola's cold words reverberated through the chiefs. By nature the Seminoles were not blood-thirsty men. They were hunters and planters. They only wanted to be left in peace.

"Fort King is several days march away," said Cowokoci. "I think we should let them march."

"Yes," added John Horse. "Let them deplete their stores. Let them grow weary."

"Then we attack," said Cowokoci. "We will track them on their march. We will make sure no supplies reach Fort King. We will make sure no reinforcements can reach them in time. Should circumstances change, we will attack when it best suits us."

Emathla listened to his son, Cowokoci. He was proud that his son was cunning. He was proud that his son possessed intelligence. He was sure that one day Cowokoci would lead the entire Nation taking the place of Micanopy when he passed. Emathla was confident that his son was up to the job.

All the chiefs agreed and General Gaines continued to Fort King unmolested.

At Fort King General Gaines was in for a shock.

"What do you mean there are no rations to be had?" he yelled at the clerk. "I have an army to feed. Men can't march on salt air alone. We need rations." He was furious. *Jackson wants this war won,* he thought, *but without supplies it cannot be done.*

"I'm sorry sir. The supplies ordered by General Scott have not arrived as of yet. We are patiently awaiting them ourselves."

General Gaines stomped from the room furiously. He quickly dispatched a packhorse train to General Clinch who was still at Fort Drane to borrow what he could. At least the news that General Clinch was safe was a relief. That was one concession. He waited at the fort for the pack horses to return.

When the men returned they had only twelve thousand rations, a small portion of what was needed to feed an army. General Gaines was very angry. He was mad at himself for coming to Florida and he was angry over the lack of organization in the Florida campaign. He had never liked General Scott. In fact, their relationship was downright hostile, and he blamed Scott's incompetence on this situation. With no other option, General Gaines ordered his men to march back to Fort Brooke to return to the west. They left Fort King the morning of February twenty-sixth in three columns marching about one hundred yards apart. The next day, they reached the Withlacoochee and the sight of the Dade massacre.

Twenty-two

In the meantime, the entire force of the Seminole nation was convening in Wahoo Swamp near the Cove of the Withlacoochee. Osceola was now the undisputed war chief in charge. John Horse and Cowokoci were figuratively and literally by his side.

"Our scouts have reported that General Gains is marching this way," said John Horse.

"When will he arrive?" asked Cowokoci.

"Tomorrow morning if they keep at the current pace," reported John Horse. "He has some rations he got from General Clinch but not nearly what he needs to get back to Fort Brooke."

Osceola listened. He asked, "How many warriors are here and ready to fight?"

"Ote Emathla reports that he has over a thousand sticks at this point and more warriors arrive each hour," said Cowokoci. It was the habit of the Seminoles to carry small sticks in their pouches. When a warrior arrived at a place ready to fight, he took a stick from his pouch and gave it to a designated counter. This is how the Seminoles kept track of the warriors in a fight. When the fight was over, each warrior gave another stick to the counter. The difference in the number of sticks before and after the battle determined how many warriors were killed or captured.

"This is good," said Osceola. "We can hold them down here while they slowly starve."

"Perhaps that will make them cooperative," said John Horse. "Maybe their father in Washington will listen and understand that we are a foe that cannot be defeated."

"I do not trust the white man's word at all," said Osceola. "We cannot live here in peace with the white man. The white man must leave these sacred grounds." John Horse and Cowokoci agreed. "We will attack when General Gaines reaches the battleground where we defeated General Clinch. This is unsettled ground and will be bad medicine for the white soldiers."

"Good," added John Horse. "It gives us the advantage with the swamp behind us. We can trap the men in the same place we trapped General Clinch."

They all nodded in agreement. They were confident General Gaines would be easily defeated.

General Gaines arrived at the Cove of the Withlacoochee right on schedule. The Indians watched from the southern side of the river as his men struggled to find the crossing.

"I think we can cross here General," yelled Lieutenant James Izard. He entered the water. "It's not too deep here."

General Gaines rode toward the lieutenant. Just as he dismounted his horse at the edge of the river, a shot rang out from the opposite shore. Lieutenant Izard fell in the water cut down by a Seminole bullet. He was quickly pulled to shore.

"Fall back! Fall back!" yelled General Gaines as the full force of the Seminole Nation opened fire upon the troops. "Prepare to defend," he ordered. The soldiers ducked behind trees. The Indians fired continuously.

And they did so for seven hours.

"Make a breastwork. Quickly men," yelled General Gaines. The men cut down trees and stacked them upon each other three high. The soldiers hid in the square enclosure. General Gaines took a breath. "Ok. I think this enclosure will keep us safe until reinforcements arrive. I've dispatched a man to General Clinch informing him that we need reinforcements. In the meantime we will defend this fort which I christen Fort Izard in honor of our brave fellow there." He pointed to Captain Izard who was suffering badly. The fatal ball entered his left eye but did not kill him immediately; he lingered five hours. He moaned in blinding pain unnerving the soldiers in close proximity.

Osceola shouted orders to the Seminoles on the opposite shore. He ordered Cowokoci to cross the river upstream with a force of braves and John Horse to cross downstream with the Black Seminoles. The Indians fired upon the haphazardly-made Fort Izard from three sides trapping the army within the breastwork.

And this went on for eight days.

Some of the Seminoles were actually enjoying the fight. "That small breastwork is no barrier to us," laughed Cowokoci. "It is already peppered with Seminole shot. Besides it is only three logs high. Any man can step right over it." They all laughed. Cowokoci got an idea. "Let us burn them out!" he shouted.

Some of the braves caught his enthusiasm. One brave ran dangerously close to the fort and set fire to the grass. The Indians observing this cheered. Hoots and hollers and laughter rang from the grasses and trees. The soldiers observed and panic ran through Fort Izard. From behind the breastwork and staying crouched, the soldiers shoveled sand over the wall to douse the fire. If a soldier lifted his head too high, he was shot. Finally the winds changed and the fire moved back toward the Indians.

"The fire has changed direction," yelled John Horse.

"Fall back," yelled Osceola. "Beat out the fire!" he ordered.

The Indians pounced on the fire lest it destroy their cover and nullify this advantage. They could move through the grasses without detection, and they did so to spy on the makeshift fort. Indians moved close enough to hear the conversations of the soldiers. After the fire was out, the Indians retreated to their camp.

"That was not a well thought out move," said Osceola. "Cowokoci, you are too impetuous at times."

Cowokoci nodded in agreement. He did not smile.

"Those braves acted to impress you. You must be more thoughtful in your words and actions."

Cowokoci said nothing.

"We do not have to work this hard," said John Horse. "If we just hold the soldiers down, they will starve."

The Seminoles felt little pressure. They took turns holding down the army. They fired their guns just enough to keep the men cowered beneath the breastworks. While the soldiers slowly starved, the Seminoles were rested and fed.

"They've just slaughtered a mule," reported John Horse.

"Hunger makes a man desperate," said Abiaka. "Soon they will be out of shot and powder too."

"I am tired of this fighting," said Micanopy. The Seminoles were not used to a prolonged siege. Their method of fighting was to hit and run. Micanopy was still chief but the spirit of the rebellion was embodied in Osceola. The warriors listened to him and he was relentless in his goal of defeating and killing every white man in Florida including all the men held down at the moment in the same place that Major Dade fell.

"Another decisive victory should convince the soldiers that they cannot win," said Osceola.

"Yes, but if we let these men leave after so much suffering, the message is that we could have killed them all and showed mercy," countered Micanopy.

"And you think that would make a difference to them? Do you really think the white father in Washington cares if his children suffer in Florida? If he did they would have rations but they don't, do they?" asked Osceola. "No," he added. "I say kill them all. Kill every invader to this land."

"I do understand both arguments," said Abraham. "To let these men leave so they can tell the tale of our superior force and how they suffered at our hands might be a smart tactic.

"True," said John Horse. "Dead men cannot talk."

"No," said Osceola. "Dead men tell tales of horror." John Horse shook his head in agreement. He understood Osceola's position. He sided with Osceola as always. Osceola was his best shot at protecting his people. He was unwavering in the fight for freedom. He could never be sure if Micanopy might compromise to end the fighting.

"If these men return to tell their tale of suffering all the white people will hear and be afraid to come here," said John Caesar.

"John Caesar is right," said Micanopy. "I think more can be achieved by showing we have the power and the force and can choose when to use it."

"I want to continue the siege until the men starve to death," said Osceola. "We are not suffering here. We can last here for many days."

"Do we have any report of reinforcements coming for the soldiers?" asked Ote Emathla. "That could change things."

"Our spies tell us that a man did make it to General Clinch. Clinch requested permission from General Scott to help and Scott said no," said John Horse.

"Are you serious?" asked Ote Emathla. "They refuse to help their own soldiers? Do these men have any loyalty to their brothers?"

"No, they don't," said Osceola. "That's exactly why they must be destroyed. If they do not honor each other, they will never honor us."

"Why would they not come to help?" asked Micanopy.

"Evidently there is bad blood between General Scott and General Gaines. They do not like each other," said John Horse. "Scott is mad that Gaines is even here."

"What of Clinch?" asked Abraham.

"He is upset. He wants to come but General Scott said no." The Seminoles shook their heads in disbelief. "I guess their orders mean more than doing what might be right—to help their fellow soldiers. Oh well. It works to our advantage anyway."

General Clinch was in a quandary. He didn't know what to do. He did not want to sit by idly while American soldiers were in battle with the Seminole when he could help. His dilemma was that General Scott outranked him and was his superior and he was bound to obey his orders. However General Gaines outranked him also and he had requested that he come.

"This is maddening," General Clinch said to his orderly. "I cannot stand by while American soldiers are being cut down by Indian rifles."

"Yes sir, it is a problem," agreed the orderly. The guns from the battle could be heard by General Clinch and all the soldiers stationed at Fort Drane. Every crack of a rifle was unnerving to all in the fort. Each bullet could be ending the life of an American soldier and most likely was. The scout sent by General Gaines said the company was being held down by the Seminoles.

"Send another dispatch to Scott requesting permission to proceed to Gaines's position." General Clinch waited all day stewing in his indecision. Finally by evening he decided that he was caught between two generals feuding like children and he would do what is right. He defied General Scott's orders to remain at Fort Drane and ordered his troops to prepare to march.

Meanwhile, contrary to Osceola's opinion, John Caesar took Micanopy's lead and contacted Gaines for a parlay.

"Hello," hollered John Caesar.

"Yes," answered Colonel Twiggs from behind the breastworks. He was another soldier regretting his pledge to fight. He was a little spooked and ducked lower behind the barrier because he did not know from what direction the voice came. It simply came out of the night.

"The Seminole are tired of fighting. We want to make peace. We want to tell you our demands and let you leave our land," said John Caesar.

Colonel Twiggs was so weary that John Caesar's voice was a welcome sound. He relaxed a little. "Come in the morning under the white flag and we will talk peaceably." If he wasn't so tired and hungry, he might have smiled.

The next morning John Caesar and a small delegation of Seminole came within two hundred yards of Fort Izard. Captain Ethan Allen Hitchcock and two others met them.

"We come in peace," said John Caesar. We are tired of fighting. We can hold you here until you starve to death but that is such a hard death. The Seminole are not so cruel."

"Any death in the duty of our country is honorable to us," replied Captain Hitchcock showing a hardline. He then added, "But we are ready to hear your requests."

"The Seminole only want to live in peace on our land without problems from men who wish to kidnap our people for slavery. The Seminole want to live in peace without American soldiers threatening our families."

"It is the desire of the American government that you leave these lands and go west. Any Indian who resists will be killed."

"We understand your position. Although you and your men will be victims of this war with this attitude. We are in the superior position and you will all die as the others before you did if you do not agree to talk peace."

"I will relay your message to General Gaines."

"And I will take your message to council. We will meet later this afternoon," said John Caesar. And the two delegations departed back to their respective camps.

The Indians met in council.

"I do not agree with your actions," said Osceola. "I do not want peace. I want death to all the invaders."

"I am with you Osceola," said Halpatter Tustenugee. "But we are low on powder and shot. We need to regroup and prepare for bigger battles. We have shown our force here to these soldiers. This is our third victory in a row."

"But you hear what the white men said this morning. They are starving and still demand that we leave this land."

"They are stubborn and unreasonable," added John Horse. "They do not waiver in their position even when they do not have the upper hand."

"I don't think they are very smart people," added Cowokoci. "They do not seem to comprehend their position here."

"Oh, I think they comprehend it alright. They are just powerless to defy the orders from Jackson in Washington. He does not understand the Florida war but he thinks he does. Evidently white men cannot think for themselves and rely on their leaders even when the leaders make bad choices."

"And his ignorance has cost many army soldiers' lives," said John Horse.

"And it will cost many more," added Osceola.

Halpatter Tustenugee joined the council. "I think we should proceed to Okeechobee lake and prepare for a decisive battle that will end this war. This is a small part of the army. We need to defeat the full force of the U.S. Army."

"Yes," said Osceola. "But if you cut off an arm and then another arm the body will die. It will bleed to death. Let the soldiers bleed to death."

"Let us go hear what they have to say," said John Horse. "What does it matter? We are the superior force. They cannot leave unless we let them leave this battlefield."

"True," agreed Osceola. "We will hear their talk but it is them not us who will leave Florida." All shook their heads in agreement and prepared to parlay with General Gaines. After all, someone had to be left alive to relay their demands to Washington. Even Osceola had to agree with that.

Twenty-three

"I don't like it," declared Osceola. "No matter what they say, it cannot be trusted."

"You speak truth, Osceola," said Micanopy. "Perhaps by talking, we can learn more about our enemy."

"Micanopy speaks good logic," said Abraham.

"What do we need to learn? These men are close to starvation. What can a starving man tell us?" asked Osceola.

"A starving man is a desperate man," said John Horse. "A desperate man doesn't always know what he is saying."

"I guess you are right John Horse," conceded Osceola. "I will listen but I will not ease up on this siege."

The Seminole chiefs were ready to meet with General Gaines. Osceola, Halpatter Tustenugee, Ote Emathla, John Caesar, Abraham, and John Horse went to meet for the parlay. Due to his age Micanopy did not go. If a swift exit was necessary, Micanopy would be slow to move. Someone would have to carry him. Besides Micanopy's absence gave the chiefs time to consider what Gaines might say. Whatever was agreed upon would have to be taken to Micanopy for final approval.

The Seminoles moved to within two hundred yards of the breastwork. To the soldiers they just appeared as if from nowhere. Abraham carried a large white cloth. The others had white feathers of peace stuck in their hair.

"General Gaines," hollered the sentry. "The Seminoles are here."

While Gaines did not go out and meet the delegation of Seminole chiefs himself, he sent representatives. As he waited to hear the outcome of the talks, his orderly spoke. "Sir, why not fight our way out of this place rather than sit here and starve?" he asked.

"I fear we are greatly outnumbered. We are at a disadvantage because the enemy can see us but we cannot see them. You saw what happened to Major Dade."

"True sir," agreed the orderly.

"If we can hold them in a bunch until Clinch arrives, he can flank them and we can turn this misery into victory."

"I see sir."

"I just cannot understand why Clinch's force has not arrived." The orderly said no more and they waited for the words of the Seminole.

Captain Hitchcock and guards marched to meet the Seminole delegation. He presented Abraham with a list of demands that Abraham interpreted for the chiefs.

"This says that we must agree to meet with the government commissioners," said Abraham.

"That is no problem," said Halpatter Tustenugee. "We want to talk with your government and explain our position."

"This also says that we must agree to abide by the commissioners decisions regarding our emigration to the west," added Abraham.

"We will meet and talk," said Halpatter. "But we will not move west."

Osceola listened. He was suspicious of the white man and did not trust his talk. "We will not leave our lands," he reiterated. "It is you who must leave."

Abraham interpreted what was said to each side of the delegation.

"If the soldiers would agree to stay north of the Withlacoochee," added John Horse. "I think we can get Micanopy to agree to stay south of the Withlacoochee."

"This is a good solution," said John Caesar.

"It is not my decision," said Captain Hitchcock. "But you are reasonable men. We are reasonable men. I will relay your message to General Gaines. He will contact the general in charge of Florida and he will talk with our President Jackson."

"White men are not reasonable men," said Osceola. Abraham did not interpret his comment for the captain but Hitchcock looked at Osceola. He could not understand the words but he did understand the vile in Osceola's voice. He fully understood Osceola's position.

"The United States Government does not wish to end this war with anything but victory," said Captain Hitchcock. "President Jackson has ordered many troops to Florida. He appointed General Scott to take charge of the Florida situation. General Scott is determined to spare nothing to achieve victory."

"Major Dade thought the same thing," said Abraham. "Every side wishes to end conflict with victory but it is clear you cannot beat the Seminole. You are dangerously close to starvation. Why would this Scott expect any different end than Seminole victory?"

Captain Hitchcock stared at Abraham. He contemplated his hunger but did not reply so Abraham continued to speak to the chiefs.

"This list also says we must cease hostilities immediately," said Abraham.

"I think that is no problem," said Ote Emathla. "Micanopy is weary of this battle. He does not wish for your soldiers to suffer further. You are starving. Starvation is a bad death."

Abraham interpreted and the soldiers nodded in agreement. They were tired, hungry, and demoralized. Just as it seemed the group was reaching accord, General Clinch arrived. The Indians knew he was coming but since they were parlaying under a white flag, they did not worry about his arrival. Most were ready to cease the fight anyway. They were satisfied with their victory and saw no need for all the soldiers to die. However, Clinch misinterpreted the scene and ordered his men to shoot at the delegation. Immediately, the Seminoles melted into Wahoo swamp, and the peace talks were over.

"Cease fire," screamed General Gaines. He approached General Clinch. "Thank you for coming but we were engaged in peace talks."

"I did not realize that. I saw Indians dangerously close to the breastworks and I feared an attack," said General Clinch.

"I fear you destroyed our best hope to end this war," said General Gaines. "The Indians agreed to end hostilities until a delegation from Washington could meet to talk."

"You do not have the authority to negotiate a peace treaty," said General Clinch.

"I know," answered General Gaines. "I only negotiated a meeting. That is the first step."

"True, true," conceded General Clinch. "This war is more complicated than anyone knows. It will not end easily."

"No, it will not. It has already been very hard." agreed General Gaines. He then ordered his men to prepare to march back to Fort Drane with General Clinch.

At the same time, in the swamps at the Seminole camp, the Seminole chiefs were in a heated discussion.

"You see," said Osceola. "The white man cannot be trusted. They fired on us when we were under their white flag of peace."

"They don't even respect their own symbols," added Cowokoci.

John Horse nodded in agreement. "I do not trust anything they say. They say they will let my people be free but will they? Is that a lie too?"

"Of course it's a lie," said Osceola. "Just like when they took Morning Dew, my wife. If a white man is speaking, he is lying."

The chiefs nodded in agreement. Then Micanopy spoke. "All of this is true but we need to pretend to sue for peace. We need to pretend we are willing to listen to the white talk. This will give us time to regroup and restock our stores."

"Micanopy speaks truth," added Abraham. "If we work the white man in the right way, we can get rations from his stores."

"Anything they give to us leaves them weaker," added John Horse. "My spies tell me that the General Clinch brought his own cattle to feed General Gaines's men."

"Is the army out of rations?" asked Micanopy.

"I don't think so," replied John Horse. "I think the general in charge would not send any help to Gaines because he does not like him."

"That is typical of the white man. He puts his own ego before his duty. His duty should be to help and protect the soldiers. He is inconsistent and does not even care for his own brothers," said Osceola.

"Yes," agreed John Horse. "This Scott is in charge now. He has some plan about flanking us from three sides. I will be getting more information from the black men camped outside the fort."
"And how does he expect to surround us? We know their every move," said Ote Emathla.

"True," added Abraham. "But they don't know we know their every move."

"I think our best tactic at this point would be to harass small parties of soldiers, attacking supply trains, and avoiding any major battles until we are armed and ready," said Osceola.

"I like Osceola's plan," said John Horse. "The white man gets sick in the Florida summer. They call it the sick season. I think we can weaken them both mentally and physically with Osceola's plan."

"It is a good plan so that is what we will do," said Micanopy. As chief, he had the last word on tactics. "I'm going to return to Peliklakaha."

Abraham considered Micanopy's idea. "I think we should return to our camp at Peliklakaha but not stay there. We should keep the tribe on the move to avoid the white soldiers and slave hunters."

"You always know what is right, Abraham. I think we should keep moving to keep the soldiers moving and weary. Florida does not suit them," said Micanopy. "They are a weak race."

"This is a good plan," said Osceola. "I will take my followers and attack when it is to our advantage. We will continually harass the soldiers. John Horse, I want you to keep your followers close."

John Horse nodded. He wanted to ride with Osceola. Osceola was a good soldier and fearless in battle.

"Then let us leave this camp," said Micanopy. "The soldiers know we are near and they will come looking for us."

"It is demoralizing to expect battle as the soldiers will be eager for it and to be let down because the enemy is nowhere in sight," said Abraham. "Our victory over the white man is made easier if we fight smart with our heads."

All the chiefs agreed with Abraham's insight. They agreed to continue skirmishing when it was to their advantage.

"Our rifles are more accurate than the American soldier rifles," said Cowokoci. "It is best to fight from afar, from the other side of the river bank is best."

"Yes," said John Horse. "When we fight in hand-to-hand combat, the odds of victory are fifty/fifty, but if we stay at a distance, the odds are in our favor. Our rifles shoot farther and are more accurate than the soldier's muskets."

"This is all true," said Osceola. "Therefore we will engage in battle and when the cannon is fired signaling the soldiers to attack with bayonets and engage in hand-to-hand combat, we will retreat to the swamps where the white man cannot follow. This will keep the white soldier frustrated and our casualties low."

The chiefs agreed and prepared to retreat to their respective camps. It was also a good idea and the desire of Micanopy to keep the tribe separated so if there was a white victory, it would be a small one, and not cripple the entire Seminole Nation. These policies and the smart battlefield tactics had the Seminoles at an advantage at this point. They controlled the peninsula of Florida. They knew every move of the U.S. Army. For these reasons, President Jackson was frustrated and he wanted victory and he wanted it immediately and he wanted it at any cost.

Twenty-four

General Winfield Scott received much criticism for not coming to the aid of General Gaines. Nevertheless President Jackson left him in charge of the Florida campaign. His plan included a three-pronged attack. He explained his plan to his commanders.

"I will march down the right side of the state with my force of regulars and Louisiana Volunteers. We will head for the Withlacoochee battle site. The Seminoles seem to favor this area and will probably be nearby."

Colonel William Lindsay and Brevet Brigadier General Abraham Eustis listened intently awaiting their assignments.

"Bill," said General Scott to Colonel Lindsay. "I want you to take your command which I believe is two-hundred and forty regulars and the Alabama militia and march to the Chocachatti in Big Hammock." Scott pointed to the map laid out in front of them. He moved his pointer down the map showing Colonel Lindsay his path. The commanders leaned in examining the map intently.

"Abraham," Scott said to General Eustis. "I want you to take your command of two hundred regulars and the militia and march down the left. Cross the St. John's River at Volusia and head to Peliklakaha. It's sometimes called Black Town. We believe this is the new headquarters for Micanopy."

General Eustis nodded his understanding and compliance. He thought that if he could capture Micanopy, the war would end. *This would be a feather in my cap*, he thought. *It would further my military career.*

"Yes sir," said General Eustis. "Capturing Micanopy would certainly help to end the war. Osceola might be the war-spirit but Micanopy is still the chief of the Seminole Nation."

"True, true," said General Scott. "We will begin March twenty-fifth. The three columns will flank the Indians and end this war once and for all."

"So be it," said Colonel Lindsay. "So be it."

The men left the meeting confident. They felt the warm Florida sunshine dispelling the cool of the early morning and thought it a good omen. They paid no notice of the man serving them coffee during their meeting. He was a black man, a slave from the burned out plantation Bulow Villa. He had listened intently to the plan. They also did not notice when he slipped into the woods to meet John Caesar who would relay the message to John Horse who would inform Cowokoci and Osceola.

"Finally, a plan that will end this mess," said General Eustis. "I like it."

"I do too," said Colonel Lindsay. "This is the first comprehensive plan. We will corner and capture the hostiles and we will all be heroes."

"Yes," agreed General Eustis.

And that is what they believed. However what they did not know, or refused to believe, was that the Seminoles knew every move of the army. They tracked and followed and only attacked when it was to their advantage. The Seminoles were familiar with the Florida scrub. It was their home and they thrived in it. The soldiers on the other hand could barely tolerate it. A brave could be within two feet of a soldier and that soldier was never aware of him. Soldiers often passed within yards of hiding Seminoles and never detected them, but the plan was in place and everyone in the army was confident the war would soon end. It's what they had to believe to survive.

The Seminoles were also planning their next moves. They met in council shortly after the general explained his plan to his commanders.

"Eustis has left St. Augustine heading for Mosquito Inlet. He is stopping every twenty miles to build houses out of block," said John Horse.

"Why would he do that?" asked Micanopy.

"My spies tell me he is building these small forts to make the transport of supplies to the south easier," replied John Horse.

"Then we'll just blow them up!" said Cowokoci.

"Nothing these soldiers do makes sense to me," said Micanopy. "Why build buildings that we can easily, as Cowokoci says, blow up? Besides they will have to leave soldiers to guard all the houses. These soldiers will be vulnerable alone in the wilderness."

The chiefs laughed. They knew Micanopy told of the obvious. They did not understand the soldier's ways.

"I will attack Eustis," said Cowokoci. "We should harass them all along the way."

"Yes," said Osceola. "We should inflict casualties whenever possible."

"The men will be tired from marching and building," added Abraham. "We should divide and harass each part of the army as they move south looking for us. They will think we are everywhere at once."

"You are correct, Abraham," said Micanopy. The chiefs nodded approval.

"I will take my followers and attack the soldiers at the Fort Defiance," said Osceola.

"Chief," said John Horse addressing Micanopy. "We need to move to strange places. The army thinks you are at Peliklakaha."

"The army will never surprise me. I will move south out of harm's way."

"I believe that is good," said John Horse. The Seminoles broke camp and proceeded to places of safety."

Twenty-five

As planned, under Scott's orders, the three army divisions began marching toward the Withlacoochee. The Seminoles tracked each division as they moved through the dense Florida scrub. Whenever the opportunity arose, the Seminoles attacked small groups of the soldiers. General Eustis was harassed most of the way.

General Eustis left for Volusia on March twenty-second. He marched toward the Withlacoochee as ordered by General Scott. When his company reached the St. Johns, he ordered the men to cross and set up camp. Their first stop would be Peliklakaha, the camp where Micanopy was reported to be. However the Seminoles were close by. Several braves were in the trees watching the soldiers cross the river and prepare their camp.

Cowokoci rode into the make-shift camp that had been set up to be close to General Eustis when he crossed the St. John's River. "What is going on with General Eustis?" he asked.

"He's been building the small forts every twenty miles. His men are quite weary and it seems he does not have the respect of his soldiers," said John Horse.

"I am not surprised by that."

"His soldiers think he is a tyrant. Some of the soldiers think they are of higher rank and expect to be treated with special favors. General Eustis treats all his soldiers the same, so as a result, many dislike him. These white people have funny notions," said John Horse. "How did you do at Fort McCrea?"

"Not bad. We trapped several soldiers between their sugar house and the fort. We killed three but could only secure two scalps before the soldiers from the fort came to their rescue. It was enough to keep the soldiers' nerves on edge though. As far as they know, we are still outside waiting to attack again so they stay inside."

"We have braves in the trees watching General Eustis prepare to cross the river. At some point we will ambush."

"Good. My goal is to harass him the entire way. Have we heard how the other two parts of the army are doing?"

"Yes. They are pretty much just walking around the scrub lost. They keep firing off the cannon hoping to find each other. Do they not know that we can hear the cannon too?"

Cowokoci shook his head in disbelief. "I think our plan is working. Just let them wear themselves out."

"Yes. The three divisions have been hacking their way through the scrub making little progress. The soldiers are wet and tired and fighting among themselves a lot."

A young brave came into camp and announced that the army was now on both sides of the river.

"Now would be a good time to attack," said John Horse.

"Then let us go," said Cowokoci. They rode toward the crossing. "Woop, woooop, wooop," he yelled and the Indians opened fire on the soldiers.

A dozen soldiers fell in the first volley. Three died. The skirmish went on for a short while. As more and more soldiers joined the fight, the Seminoles melted back into the Florida scrub taking their wounded with them, as they always did. Five braves were hit, three were in danger of dying. The women in camp immediately tended to the wounded when the Seminoles returned from the fight.

When the Indians were gone, the soldiers continued crossing the river and setting up a camp. This took four days. Finally the entire force under the direction of General Eustis was on the same side of the river. General Eustis ordered the army to continue toward Peliklakaha where he hoped to find Micanopy, where he hoped to capture the leader and end this war once and for all.

Meanwhile back in camp the Seminoles were in council. They were appraising their actions and deciding on their next move.

"I think we need to continue to harass General Eustis as he attempts to get to Peliklakaha," said Emathla.

"I agree with you, father," said Cowokoci.

"But," interjected Yaha Hadjo. "We need to be more careful. We have three braves in very bad condition from this recent skirmish and they will probably die."

"War is serious business," said John Horse. "Any moment could be our last."

"You speak true words," said Emathla.

"We did not ask for this war," said Cowokoci.

"No we did not," agreed John Horse. "This was forced upon us and the death of both Indians and soldiers rests on the shoulders of their President Jackson. He sits in Washington ordering war without concern for the consequences."

"It does seem so," said Emathla. "Why does *he* not come to talk? Maybe he has reasons we do not know. Maybe we would understand better if the soldiers made sense in their talks."

"There is no sense in white men so their talk can have no sense either," said Cowokoci.

"The sick season is coming," said John Horse. "So the soldiers are anxious to complete this latest campaign.

"Sick season. What a laugh," said Cowokoci. "White men are weak. Our women are more resilient than the white soldiers. Sick season. We never heard of a sick season before the white people came to our land."

"They are an odd race," said Yaha Hadjo. "If the sunshine and heat of the Florida summer are too much for them, why do they continue to come?"

"It is a mystery," said Emathla.

A young brave rode into camp and signaled to John Horse. John Horse left the council and talked with the boy. When he returned to the circle, he informed the chiefs of the latest information on General Eustis.

"Eustis has finally crossed the river and he is now headed to where the Ocklawaha and the Withlacoochee meet," said John Horse. "I think we should attack when he reaches that point."

"He will have to camp there. It will take a while to get his army across the river," said Emathla.

"That is a good place," said Yaha Hadjo. "We will have the advantage there."

"Has Micanopy evacuated Peliklakaha?" asked Emathla.

"Yes," replied John Horse. "He has been gone for over a week now."

"Good. Eustis is exhausting his men trying to get through the thick scrub for no reason. No Indians are there," said Emathla. He laughed.

"Yes and even his horses are dropping dead from exhaustion. He has lost several so far," reported John Horse. "The white soldiers are really not cut out for this land and neither are their animals. Maybe that's why they steal Seminole animals." He laughed thinking of his cattle.

Cowokoci said, "Then we attack when he arrives at the river. Probably tomorrow." All nodded in agreement. The next day, the Seminoles prepared for the ambush. They painted themselves for war. They filled their bandoleer bags with shot and powder and headed to meet General Eustis once more. The Seminoles tied up their horses a quarter of a mile from the river crossing. They crept up on foot to survey the area.

"What are they doing?" asked Yaha Hadjo?

"Looks like they are building a bridge," said John Horse.

"That seems like an awful waste of time," said Yaha Hadjo.

"They can't get their wagons across any other way," said John Horse.

"That is exactly why we can track them so easily," said Cowokoci. "They take so long to get anywhere. When they aren't marching, they are shooting off cannons to find each other."

John Horse laughed.

"You ready?" asked Yaha Hadjo. "Then let's go."

Cowokoci let out a war cry and the Seminoles stepped from the scrub and opened fire.

It was a hot day and the soldiers were sweating and miserable. They were constructing a large raft-like structure to place in the river when they heard Cowokoci's war cry. Confusion ran through the ranks.

"Take cover," yelled General Eustis. He was sitting on his horse. He slid to the ground and took cover behind a tree. "Bring up the cannon," he yelled.

The Seminoles fired a great volley of shots and filled the area with gun smoke. It was hard to see where anyone was at that point. A bullet caught Yaha Hadjo and he fell to the ground. He was bleeding profusely. John Horse grabbed him under his arms and dragged him into the dense woods. With Yaha Hadjo down, the Seminoles began to fall back. As they left the area, they noticed several soldiers lifeless on the ground.

Back in camp, the Seminoles mourned the loss of Yaha Hadjo.

"He was a good warrior," said Emathla.

"Yes," said John Horse. "I will take him to his family for his final preparations."

"Yes that is proper," said Emathla.

"This is what war is about," said Cowokoci. "Good men die."

"Yes, my son," said Emathla. "I think we should go to the main force of the Nation and talk with the other chiefs. We should plan our next move. Eustis will continue to Peliklakaha where he will find nothing."

"I think we should continue to attack," said Cowokoci. "I want revenge for the loss of Yaha Hadjo."

"You will have your revenge," said Emathla. "Just on another day. This latest campaign of the white soldiers has been a failure. Most of the soldiers are sick."

"Which is why we should push hard now," argued Cowokoci.

"Patience my son. We just lost a good friend. Let us regroup for a short while."

General Eustis continued to Peliklakaha. When he was close, he sent an advance guard to appraise the danger in the area.

"Soldier, stealthily ride ahead and check out the situation," ordered the General.

"Yes sir," replied the soldier and he quickly rode ahead of the army. "Why me?" he thought. "I'm a sitting duck out here in front of the very noisy army. It's not like they can't hear us coming." He dismounted several hundred yards from Micanopy's town and went through the scrub hoping not to be detected. He was very surprised and relieved to find the town deserted. He quickly went back to his unit.

"What did you find, private?" asked General Eustis.

"Sir, I didn't find anything. The place is deserted."

"What? That can't be. Let us proceed quickly," he ordered. When the army reached Peliklakaha, General Eustis was angry. "How can this be? Army Intelligence said Micanopy was here."

"It appears they have been gone for several weeks," said a Colonel Goodwyn.

"Yes, it does appear that way. This campaign is a total failure. We don't know where the enemy is or what they are doing or planning." He spat in the dirt and stomped off. The soldiers were poking around the village. There was nothing to be found but empty abandoned chickee huts. "Burn everything," General Eustis ordered. "Burn everything," he yelled. He was frustrated at the difficulty of this march that produced no results but to wear out his command.

General Scott's campaign did nothing to end the war. President Jackson was upset over the fiasco and he demanded an explanation from General Scott. General Scott was forced to defend his actions in the Florida campaign. He was relieved of duty and recalled to Washington D.C.

"Sir," said Scott, addressing the President. "I don't think anyone realizes the immense space that the U.S. troops had to traverse. Most of my volunteer troops were soon completing their term of duty and were therefore reluctant to fight so close to going home. This was exacerbated by the fact that the supplies were slow to arrive. I was expected to traverse wild country, but the wagons I ordered did not arrive until March. By that time, the sick season was starting to come on us. The lack of clear water and limited rations caused much sickness among the troops. The heat was unbearable and men from cold climates were unable to tolerate it. Furthermore, the citizens of Florida were more of a hindrance than a help. They imagined an Indian at every turn. And General Gaines's intrusion hindered the supply lines as well."

President Jackson listened in silence. He was quite perturbed with the Florida campaign. He has spent unprecedented sums of money to capture Florida and his political foes were demanding accountability. He needed to win this war so he could sell Florida land grants and recoup much of the money.

"I have written a detailed report," continued General Scott. "I will present it to the Court of Inquiry."

The Court of Inquiry after much testimony found that General Scott was diligent in his duties and did no wrong. They further found that the climate, lack of supplies, communication, and soldiers—either attitude of or lack thereof—contributed to the failure of his campaign. He was exonerated but President Jackson was not happy. This war was quickly becoming a political liability. Next he appointed Major General Thomas S. Jesup to take command of the Florida situation. President Jackson was now desperate. He had nearly depleted his supply of generals. General Jesup was his last hope. He obliquely expressed his desperation. The message received was to capture Osceola and end this war at all costs. At this point, the Seminoles appeared to be everywhere at once. They controlled most of the state of Florida. President Jackson was desperate and desperate times calls for desperate measures.

General Jesup took over with a vengeance. His first invasion captured forty-one Black Seminoles from a village at the headwaters of the Ocklawaha. He asked neighboring states for twelve-month volunteers. He bragged that with one thousand men he would have this war over in sixty days. Unfortunately though he had another thing coming.

Twenty-six

The Navy came to the aid of General Jesup. Sailors took over the forts and patrolled the waterways. This action allowed deployment of all the soldiers to actively search for Seminoles. General Jesup was somewhat successful in his first year of command. In January of eighteen thirty-seven, he captured sixteen Black Seminoles from Osceola's band in the Panosufkee Swamp. He kept on the move and captured or killed Seminoles all over the territory. In a little over a month, he had the Seminoles on the run. They could not plant corn and the loss of property was very hard on the tribe, but they were far from giving up. An advance U.S. Army scouting party discovered a settlement just north of Lake Okeechobee on Hatchalustee Creek.

"General, we have discovered a major camp. The Seminoles are unaware that we have found them."

"Good work, sergeant," said General Jesup. We will divide into two columns. One column will attack the warriors, and the other will attack and seize the Seminole baggage train attempting to flee. If we hold their woman and children, they may be more compliant to our wishes."

"Yes sir," agreed the sergeant and the Army put the plan into action.

"Run," screamed an Indian woman to her children. "Leave everything and escape," she commanded. Her children were reluctant to run. The soldiers were holding their mother. She kicked and bit but the soldiers held her. Her son fled into the dense Florida scrub but her daughter remained with her and was captured. General Jesup's troops captured one hundred horses on that day. They also took prisoner many of the women and children while the warriors fought on the other shore. The ones that escaped were left without blankets, cookware, and their stores of food. The warriors put up a good fight in typical Seminole fashion. They returned fire, retreated a distance just out of range of the U.S. Army rifles, turned and fired on the troops again. When the soldiers advanced so that the Indians were in range of their rifles, the Indians retreated again. This went on until dark when the soldiers gave up and returned to their base camp on the north end of Lake Tohopekaliga. The warriors set up a makeshift camp when the soldiers stopped pursuing.

"This was a surprise," said John Horse. "Why didn't we know they were in the area?"

"I don't know," said Abraham. "We will need better information. We need more young braves out scouting."

"Yes, this was bad," said Cowokoci. "This was very bad. We lost cattle, horses, and most importantly gun powder."

As they talked, escaped woman and children made it to their camp. There were but a few. "They took my mother," cried one young brave.

"Be brave," said John Horse. He patted the boy's shoulder. "Your mother will be fine. They won't harm her. In fact they will feed her."

"He's right," confirmed Cowokoci. "We are ready to send young braves to check on them and see what is happening with the soldiers. Would you like to go with them?"

The boy shook his head yes and put on a brave face. He was scared, but felt comforted at having found the camp. He ran like his mother told him and found himself lost in the scrub. He searched a while for his sister, and decided he should find the camp. The soldiers probably had his sister too. *She would be better off with our mother anyway*, he thought at the time. "Yes," he said. "I would like to go. I want to make sure my sister is with my mother, and not wandering in the woods somewhere."

"Then you may go," said Abraham. "Just be very careful."

When the boys were near the army camp, they tied their horses in a sheltered spot in the scrub. They sneaked up, being very careful to be quiet. They hid in the brush until they could melt into the camp as if they had been captured before. The young brave found his mother. She hugged him to her. He noticed his sister asleep on the ground next to his mother.

"I was afraid but I ran like you said. I looked for a long time for my sister. I see she is with you."

"Yes my son. She didn't run."

"She is better with you. I was sent to spy. I am to return with news of your safety. Did anyone hear what the soldiers are up to?"

"Yes. They think as long as they have the women and children, the warriors will be easier to deal with. They think they can hold us hostage."

"Why don't you leave with me now?" he asked.

"Because we can't all leave. They will notice. Besides they took our food. As long as we are here, we will be fed and clothed. Our warriors will rescue us when it best serves the tribe. In the meantime we will eat up whatever we can of the white man's food."

"Do the chiefs know of this plan?"

"It has been mentioned in council before. We will hinder the army's movement and spy on them. They do not know that some of our black Seminole women speak their English. They think only a few of the men do, and so they talk in front of us. We smile and listen for whatever information we can use against them."

"So you think you are fine for the time being?" he asked.

"Yes," she said. "You are very brave for coming here to check on us. Go now and report what you see. Be strong my son."

The brave boy sneaked out of the fort the same way he sneaked in. The soldiers paid little attention to the young children. He met the other spies at the horses and they headed back to camp to report what they saw and heard. John Horse smiled when he saw them return.

"You have fulfilled your mission," he told them when they returned. "The tribe is proud." The boys beamed. They told everything they saw and heard.

"They have Ben," said one young brave. "They are going to let him leave to negotiate a talk. However they are keeping his family as hostage."

"That's right," said another young spy. "He should be here tomorrow to tell the soldiers demands."

"That is good information," said John Horse.

"We already know their demands," said Osceola. "They want us to leave. I will never leave."

"I've said it before and I'll say it again, neither will I," said John Horse.

"This Jesup thinks he has the upper hand. He has only captured women and children," said Emathla.

"True, true," said Cowokoci. "Let him feed them a while. Then we will free them. After all he has our cattle. Let them eat up our cattle before we take them back."

"That is good thinking," said John Horse. "They never did pay me for the cattle they stole from me!"

"Don't hold your breath on that," laughed Cowokoci. "If a white man is promising something, he is lying!"

"Maybe we should send the rest of the women and children to surrender. They will be fed and clothed. This will leave us to the business of war without distractions," suggested John Horse.

"That is something to think about," responded Emathla. "These soldiers think they have it all under control, but we will teach them differently."

The next day Ben arrived as expected. "I come from Jesup. He is holding our families."

"Is he treating them well?" asked Emathla.

"Yes he is. He thinks we cannot rescue them from his fort, but I can see the soldiers pay little attention. There are always guards on watch duty but not more than we can overpower quietly," said Ben. "They are making me come back because they are holding my family hostage."

"What does he expect of you?" asked Emathla.

"He wants the chiefs to meet and talk with him."

"Talk is useless," said Osceola. He was angry and it could be heard in his voice. Osceola was always angry at the thought of more talks.

"How do we know we can trust that General Jesup is being honest?" asked Emathla.

"The answer to that is easy," said Osceola. "We know we cannot trust him."

"I will go and speak first," said Abraham. "We will see if they let me enter and leave their camp."

"They could send you to slavery," said John Horse.

"That is why you and several warriors will be waiting outside of their camp to rescue me if they try to spirit me off to the north."

"I could do that," said John Horse. "I would make certain that none of the slave hunters would live long enough to deliver you to Georgia."

"Then it is settled," said Emathla. "Ben go back and say we are coming. Don't be specific about when. Abraham you will be the first to go in. John Horse and my son Cowokoci will gather warriors and wait for your safe exit from the camp."

"We will insure your safe return," said Cowokoci.

"Yes we will," said John Horse.

"Ben, when in the soldier camp, find out everything you can about the soldiers and their plans. We will send young braves as messengers to hear what you learn," said Emathla. "We will use this recent victory for General Jesup to our advantage."

"I will pay attention to everything in camp," assured Ben. "Also, I think this General Jesup is different from the previous generals. He has paid attention to our tactics of hitting the enemy and dispersing before we have casualties. He intends to do the same to us."

"We have noticed a different set of tactics from the soldiers lately," said Cowokoci. "They are patrolling in smaller scouting parties."

"That is the plan," said Ben. "It seems he has figured out that large armies are very easy for us to track."

"We will use this information to our advantage," said Emathla. "Be safe Ben and keep us informed."

"I will." Then he turned to Abraham. "Abraham, General Jesup is trying to separate the black and red Seminoles. He has offered freedom for me and my family if I cooperate with him and move west."

"He says a lot of things. This Jesup can be deceitful," said Abraham. "You could find yourself a slave on some far-off plantation."

"I am very aware of that," said Ben. "I just want to be honest and tell everything. General Jesup said that any Black Seminole that comes in is guaranteed freedom for himself and his family."

"I don't think I believe him," said John Horse. "But even if I did, I am Seminole and I will fight to the death to be free in my homeland." Everyone agreed.

Ben reappeared a few days later bearing gifts from Jesup. "General Jesup has sent this tobacco," said Ben. "He wants me to persuade the chiefs to meet and parlay."

"It has already been decided that Abraham will go in first," said Osceola. "Even if he is not sincere about talks and this is a trick, we don't think he will kill Abraham. He is too valuable as a slave."

"So far General Jesup has left the Black Seminoles in the detention camp alone. He has not allowed slave hunters to come close to them."

"That is how it seems. We need to be sure he is not just biding his time at the moment," said John Horse.

"We must be very cautious," said Emathla. "Abraham I think you should test the waters in the next couple of days. Go when you feel the signs are right."

Abraham shook his head in agreement. "I will go in two days." Abraham spent the next two days thinking and meditating. He was nervous regarding General Jesup's intentions. *I feel secure in having John Horse and Cowokoci close by, but if Jesup intends to imprison or kill me, there is little they could do*, he thought. Finally, the night before he was to go, he informed John Horse. "I will go tomorrow," he said.

John Horse shook his head in agreement. "I will tell Cowokoci and we will accompany you."

"They might kill me on the spot."

"I don't think so. If they would do something like that, all negotiations would cease. There would be no need for talks after that. Jesup is a smart man. He knows this."

"That is true. Smoke a pipe with me. I have some of General Jesup's tobacco here. John Horse sat with Abraham and they talked late into the night. Abraham wanted John Horse to know that he is to take his place should things go wrong. "You are a good warrior and a good leader. Our people will follow you." The next morning they mounted their horses and rode toward the army camp. When they were close, they tied up their horses in a safe hiding place and moved closer on foot.

"I guess this is it," said Abraham. "If anything happens to me, take revenge on General Jesup please."

"Don't worry about that," said Cowokoci. "We will not rest till General Jesup is dead."

"We will be close," said John Horse. They watched Abraham disappear down the path toward the Army camp.

Abraham reached the edge of the camp. Soldiers were milling about. Many were sitting around casually chatting. Abraham took in the scene quickly, picked out the tent that was obviously the headquarters of General Jesup, and with a white flag in hand, he proudly walked right through the camp. To the soldiers who were accustomed to humble slaves, Abraham seemed arrogant. Some of the volunteers from the southern states wanted to do him harm. "Is that the one we're hanging today?" said one Volunteer. Abraham heard him but ignored him and walked right up to General Jesup's tent. He planted the white flag in the dirt at the tent opening and went in.

The General was sitting at a desk examining papers. He looked up and upon seeing Abraham, he smiled. He jumped up and took Abraham's hand. He shook it vigorously.

"I am very glad you have come. Please sit down." He turned to an orderly, "Get some refreshments," he ordered. Abraham took a seat. Jesup continued. "Thank you for coming. I think as reasonable men, we can work out this unfortunate Florida situation." Abraham listened. He was curious to discover why the General was talking to him as if he were in charge of the Seminoles.

"I am a free black man. I belonged to Micanopy. I am his interpreter. He has given me freedom papers. I am not a Seminole chief."

"Maybe not, but you are advisor to Micanopy who is chief of the Seminoles."

"That is true."

"And Micanopy listens to your council. You are a reasonable man. I'm sure you will relay our talks to him." Cautiously, Abraham shook his head in agreement.

"I will guarantee that the Black Seminoles will remain with the tribe when they go west. They will be guaranteed safety for themselves and their families."

"We have been promised things before," said Abraham.

"This promise I will put in a peace treaty. I will guarantee by that treaty that the full force of the United States Government will back the treaty."

"Indians do not trust pieces of paper, especially your pieces of paper. Your great white chief has promised things before. Your government tricked us with the Treaty of Moultrie. Chiefs signed one thing and were told they signed something else later on."

"I am in charge now. The great white chief listens to me. He trusts my council."

"What is it you want from me at this time?" asked Abraham.

"I want you to bring in the chiefs for talks and a treaty. I will guarantee the Black Seminoles' safety and freedom."

"I will relay your message. I will do my best to persuade the chiefs to come in and talk." Abraham rose, shook the general's hand, took his white flag, and walked out of camp. He was very nervous as he moved through the soldiers. He was confident that General Jesup meant what he said. He just wasn't sure if he could control his soldiers. Abraham quickly met up with John Horse and Cowokoci and they silently moved toward the horses. When safely out of earshot of the soldiers' camp, he spoke.

"That was very frightening," said Abraham.

John Horse laughed. "You were very brave to walk in the midst of the soldiers. What did General Jesup have to say?"

"He wants the chiefs to meet with him for talks. He has promised that the Black Seminoles will be safe in their freedom in the west."

"That is interesting," said John Horse. "He is trying to divide the tribe. If the Black Seminoles come in and agree to emigrate, he is fighting with fewer braves in Florida."

"This General Jesup thinks he is very clever," said Cowokoci. "Does he not think we are smart and can figure out what he is trying to do?"

"He thinks the Black Seminoles are the main war force. He thinks they are fighting for their families," said Abraham.

Cowokoci laughed. "Has he not met Osceola? He will never surrender regardless of who remains with him."

"I know," said John Horse. "I will remain with him. I do not trust white men's words. It is a long trip to the west. How can he guarantee safety the entire way?"

"He can't," said Cowokoci.

Twenty-seven

Back at camp, the chiefs met in council.

"He has promised to end hostilities for the time being as long as we meet and talk and ultimately agree to abide by the agreements made during the talks," said Abraham.

"What guarantee does he give us?" asked Emathla.

"He says his word is his bond," answered Abraham.

"What does that mean?" asked Osceola. "What promise can he make without the white chief Jackson?"

"He says he is good friends with the President Jackson. He says he was given freedom to end the hostilities as he sees fit."

"What else does he say," asked John Horse.

"He promises that the Black Seminoles can stay with the tribe."

"Only if we go west," added Cowokoci.

"Yes. He is promising that we can go together and remain together."

"I don't know," said Micanopy. "What do you think Abraham? Is this General Jesup honorable?"

"As honorable as any white man, I suppose."

"That says it all," said Osceola.

"We could use some time to regroup," said Emathla. "We have been on the move so much that our women and children are weary. Our stores of food are running low. Let us meet for talks and demand rations for our people. In the meantime we can plant during the cease-fire."

"I suppose we need to be patient," said Cowokoci. "The rainy weather is wearing out the soldiers anyway. The sick season, as they call it, is coming on. It would be good to eat up some of their rations."

"This General Jesup is using different tactics from the previous soldier chiefs. It might be a good idea to slow his progress. Ceasing hostilities would do that," said John Horse.

"Abraham, go back and tell General Jesup that we will talk," said Micanopy.

When the time came for the talks, Abraham was with General Jesup. They waited all morning in camp, but no Seminole chief materialized.

"I don't understand it," said Abraham. "I'm sure they are coming. They said they would, and Indians do what they say."

"Well, then where are they?" demanded General Jesup.

"I don't know. Let me go look for them. I'm sure they are on the trail. Maybe something is wrong or someone is sick."

"Just make sure you find them or I will resume hostilities. This time I won't be playing around."

"Yes sir, I will return," assured Abraham.

Abraham found Micanopy and the other chiefs camped four miles from the soldier camp. "Why are you not coming to talk," he asked.

"How can we be sure this is not a trick?" said Emathla.

"I don't think it is. I think I trust General Jesup," said Abraham.

"That is foolish thinking," said Cowokoci.

"Perhaps," added John Horse.

"Well, what is it going to be? The soldiers are holding Ben and his family hostage to make sure I return," said Abraham. He had intended to return anyway and take General Jesup up on the offer to allow him and his family to remain free. At least he was entertaining the idea. It seemed inevitable to him that he would have to compromise at some point, and with General Jesup's offer, this seems like a good time to him. He thinks if he could convince the chiefs to join him, he won't appear to be a traitor.

"We will talk," said Micanopy. "Let us see where it leads."

And so it was decided that the Seminoles would go to the talk. However Micanopy and Osceola would not attend just in case it was a trick. Yaholoochee, Micanopy's nephew, would represent him in the talks. Osceola was ill. He had a persistent fever that returned often. Emathla and Cowokoci did not go either. With Osceola ill, Cowokoci was the leading war chief. He did not trust the talks and refused to go. John Horse went in his place.

General Jesup welcomed the chiefs. "This is a good day, gentleman. Thank you for coming." He was happy to see John Horse but noted that Micanopy and Cowokoci were missing. This troubled him, but he understood their caution. He would bide his time and build trust with them.

The Seminoles expressed their desires. They wished to stay in Florida but agreed to stay south of the Hillsborough River.

"That is a temporary solution," said General Jesup. "One I will honor for the time being, but ultimately you must agree to emigrate west."

"I don't think the tribe will agree," said Ote Emathla. He was being honest because he saw no reason to try and trick the general at this point.

"These are as generous terms as you will ever negotiate with the United States Government," said General Jesup. "All your tribe members will be safe in the move. We will pay all expenses and support the tribe in the west for twelve months after you arrive. That will give you time to plant corn and build herds."

The chiefs talked amongst themselves. Finally they decided to sign the agreement. It was time to plant for the next season, and the Indians were having a difficult time because every time they had a crop in the ground, soldiers burned it. It was agreed that Micanopy would come in and remain in the detention camp near Fort Brooks as a hostage to insure the rest of the tribe acquiesced and went along with General Jesup's demands. The chiefs were sure Micanopy would agree. The Seminoles departed to give the news to Micanopy.

"Micanopy is old and tired. He is tired of fighting. He won't mind waiting in the camp while we regroup," said John Horse.

"I think you are right," said Ote Emathla. "It is Emathla, Cowokoci, and Osceola that I'm concerned about."

John Horse laughed. "I will talk to my friends. It will be fine." The Seminoles all agreed to move south of the Hillsborough. Osceola listened to the news. He folded his arms and walked away scowling. He was not happy, but he agreed and honored the cease-fire.

Micanopy turned himself in, and slowly but steadily the tribe members joined him until there were seven hundred Indians in the detention camp near Tampa. Twenty-six ships waited in the harbor to transport them. But for supplies, they would have already been gone.

Things were going well for General Jesup. He was thrilled and bragged to Washington that he had the war concluded. The slaveholding citizens were not happy with him, but the northern part of the country felt slavery was wrong and they supported ending a war that was very costly in both lives and money. Things were looking good for General Jesup. He was feeling elated. Then things happened that were beyond his control.

"I'm telling you, General Hernandez, this is more of a slave rebellion than anything. Why can't Washington understand that?" said General Jessup.

"I don't know sir. Does the President know that nearly five hundred slaves have fled the plantations? If this news reaches the slave population in the south, it could be a disaster for the southern economy." Brigadier General Joseph Hernandez was in charge of the volunteers on the east coast. He took his orders directly from Jesup.

"I know that. But of more concern to me is Florida," General Jessup continued. "I promised freedom to any Black Seminole that comes in, and the President has refused to honor my promise."

"What are you going to do now?" said Hernandez.

"I don't know," mused Jessup. "I guess capture of the war chiefs is the only answer. We must achieve this end at all cost."

"I'm afraid you are right, Sir," Hernandez agreed, "but I don't know how we will succeed where others have failed."

"Failure is not an option," Jesup said. "We need to move Micanopy to a boat as soon as possible."

"Yes sir," replied Hernandez.

Meanwhile the Seminoles were apprised of the decision not to honor the agreement allowing the Black Seminoles to emigrate with the tribe.

"I told you this Jesup cannot be trusted," said Osceola. "He even let slavers enter the relocation camp which he expressly promised would not happen."

"When did this happen? What does this mean for Ben and Abraham?" asked John Horse.

"Probably nothing. They have their freedom papers," said Emathla.

"Like the slavers will respect a piece of paper," said Cowokoci. "General Jesup is expecting us for another talk. I will not be going."

"Obviously neither will I," said John Horse.

"The hostilities resume," said Osceola.

"First we need to empty the relocation camp of our people," said Emathla.

And that is exactly what they did. John Horse and Osceola were joined by Abiaka, the Miccosukee chief. They were camped outside the relocation camp making plans.

"It is a cloudy night," said Osceola. "There will be no moonlight. Each of us will enter at a different point and quietly alert our people."

"Are we sure they will follow us?" asked John Horse.

"My people will follow me," said Abiaka. "I'm sure most of the others respect or at least fear Osceola, so they will all follow."

"I will find Micanopy first. All will follow him," said Osceola. It was a warm balmy June night. The sea breezes were gentle. At midnight, the rescuers accompanied by two hundred Miccosukee warriors skulked into camp. Quietly they roused the detainees. Micanopy protested.

"I'm tired of fighting. I'm an old man. I just want to live in peace," he said.

Osceola gave Micanopy a stern look.

"The slavers were here. They will be back. We can talk away from here," said John Horse.

Micanopy shrugged. He knew he had no choice. He quietly stood, waved to his tribe, and the entire group of seven hundred moved silently into the Florida scrub. By morning, the camp was empty.

Jesup was incensed. "What do you mean they are gone?" he screamed.

"They appear to have left in the night."

"And no one stopped them?" he asked

"No one heard them."

"We are back to square one. I should have done more to stop the slavers. Now what do I say to Washington? I told them the war was over."

"Sir, no one could predict the treachery of the Indians in leaving the detention camp."

"It is clear to me that the Indians would prefer death to leaving this country. I'm afraid nothing short of extermination will rid us of them."

"It is just a minor setback. I'm sure you will prevail."

"No sir," replied General Jesup. "I have entirely failed. I will send a letter of resignation promptly."

General Jesup's letter of resignation was not accepted by the President; therefore, he was obliged to remain and continue with the war.

The Seminoles on the other hand had used the cease-fire to restock their supplies. They were replete with shot, powder, and food. The war was back on.

Twenty-eight

General Jesup was understandably frustrated, angry, and demoralized. This brouhaha was the only defeat of his career. He was tired of sick and complaining soldiers; he was tired of whining citizens who saw an Indian behind every bush. He was simply tired of Florida with its heat and crawling and biting bugs. Despite all of this, he was a military man of honor. If he must remain, then he would turn this defeat around. He vowed he would wait until the sick season was over and then he would use the Seminole's own war tactics against them.

Early in September General Hernandez was camped at the burned-out Bulow Plantation near St. Augustine. Fortunately for him, many of the plantation slaves were growing weary of living with the Seminoles. The thought of fleeing plantation life seemed like a good idea at the time, but the reality of living in the swamps, constantly on the move to avoid capture, and subsisting on coonti root and alligator was far from idyllic.

One particular man, John Philip, had ridden with Emathla and John Caesar. He was a strong warrior. He was not so much weary of living in the Florida scrub as he was in love with a woman who was weary of living in the Florida scrub.

"General Hernandez, I give myself up to you in the hopes that you will be generous and allow me to stay with my wife," he said.

"Your future depends on your cooperation," replied Hernandez. "What can you tell me to help me?"

"Sir, I would be inclined to cooperate with you and your cause for some guarantees."

"Very well," replied Hernandez. "What can you tell me?"

"I know the location of the camp of Emathla." He spoke quietly. He felt bad about betraying his friend, but he had to think of his future and his family.

"Excellent," said Hernandez. "General Jesup will be very glad to hear this."

The ensuing raid on Emathla's camp took place at dawn catching Emathla unaware. He was standing at the river's edge wearing only a breechcloth. But for his tiny skirt, he was naked. Alarm ran through the camp but there was nothing the Seminoles could do. The army had already surrounded them. Hernandez took the prisoners back to Bulow Plantation.

"I don't want to stay here long," said Hernandez. "I fear with such an important prisoner as Emathla, there could be quick reprisals. I'm sure his sons will come for him and they will want revenge."

"That is undoubtedly to happen, sir. He is the brother-in-law of Micanopy, head chief of the Seminoles, is he not?" asked his lieutenant.

"Yes, he is. And with Micanopy so old, he is a very important chief. The Seminoles will follow him."

"What should I tell the men?" asked his lieutenant.

"Tell them we leave for St. Augustine soon, but I want to talk to the prisoner first."

Emathla was shown to General Hernandez's makeshift office in the burned out plantation.

"King Phillip," said Hernandez calling him by the name the white men used. "It is time to give up this fight and emigrate to the west."

"The white man's time tables mean nothing to the Indian," said Emathla. "In the first treaty signed with the white man, we were given twenty years to work out our disagreements. We have many years left. The white man has not honored that."

"That is something you will have to take up with the President in Washington. I am a soldier and as a soldier I am bound to follow the orders of my superiors. My orders say capture the Indians and end this war."

"I see no reason for this fighting. This land is big enough for all of us."

"Perhaps, but those are not my orders. General Jesup is very upset over the escape of Micanopy from the detention camp in Tampa."

"I would expect him to be," agreed Emathla.

"He is embarrassed because he told the President that the war was over and the Indians would be leaving soon. For this reason he is even more determined to end this war. He will not be patient anymore."

"I understand what you are saying, but I am a prisoner here. I can do nothing to persuade my people from here."

"Pick a warrior that you trust. Send him to bring in your son, Wild Cat, for talks."

"My son Cowokoci, Wild Cat as you call him, will honor my wishes. But my wish is for him to remain free and not a prisoner like myself."

"General Jesup is very angry. He will not allow that. Who should I send to bring in your son for talks?"

"Tomoka John would be the best choice."

"Then it is done. We will be moving to St. Augustine shortly."

Tomoka John visited Cowokoci's camp first. "They have your father," he said.

"Who has my father?" asked Cowokoci.

"General Hernandez. And he has taken him to St. Augustine. They have locked him up in the stone fort. They say if you don't come in and talk, they will kill him."

"It might be a trap," said Cowokoci. "But I must go see my father and make sure he is alright." Cowokoci prepared to go to General Hernandez for an escort to his father in the fort at St. Augustine. He dressed in his finest scarlet red leggings. When he wove his best turban about his head, anchoring it with burnished silver, he added a plume of the white crane feathers of peace. When he arrived at the fort, General Jesup met him with an outstretched hand.

"Thank you for coming. Your father is anxious for you to take his message to his people."

"Is my father well?" asked Cowokoci.

"Yes. Yes. We are treating him well. He is royalty, after all," replied General Jesup.

"Thank you. I would like to see him now."

"Of course. Of course. Come this way."

Cowokoci and his father Emathla spoke privately.

"My son thank you for coming."

"Father, Tomoko John told me you would be put to death if I did not come here within two weeks."

"I don't know. General Jesup may have been bluffing."

"That is possible but I would not take a chance with your life."

When Emathla heard this, tears welled up in his eyes. Seminoles rarely show affection in public, but Emathla was overwhelmed and he hugged his son. "What is next, my son? Is General Jesup allowing you to leave?"

"Yes, for the time being. I must arrange a talk with the war chiefs. I know John Horse will attend. He has his freedom papers and should be safe from slavery. I will talk to Osceola. He respects you and will most likely attend. He is very ill with the white man's fever at the moment."

"What happens if he doesn't agree to talk?"

"General Jesup is threatening your life, but as you said it may be a bluff. I will do my best to return quickly."

"Thank you, my son. Give my best to Osceola."
Cowokoci rode from St. Augustine under the gawking stares of the citizens, but he held his head high. Many remarked at the regal nature of his presence. He looked like a prince, a majestic son of royalty.

"General Jesup," asked a lieutenant, "why did you let him leave?"

"I didn't want to," Jessup replied. "He is undoubtedly the ablest chief in the tribe. He not only has the respect as a war chief but he has the hereditary rights also."

"Yes sir. He is ruthless," agreed the lieutenant. "I think he rather enjoys the fighting."

"Yes, I think so. I let him leave because I want Osceola. He is the war spirit. I need them both," said Jessup. "If I had kept Wild Cat, Osceola would disappear. He'd never show for a talk again. The President wants Osceola at all cost."

"Sounds like the only strategy available to you," the lieutenant said.

"That's how I see it," said General Jesup.

Twenty-nine

Cowokoci rode first to John Horse.

"General Jesup is threatening to kill my father if we don't come in for a talk. He wants the escaped slaves returned," said Cowokoci holding in his anger.

"I have some people who are tired of life in the scrub," said John Horse. "I will talk to them. They will agree to return because they think the plantation life was easier. Actually this will work to their advantage because they can claim they were captives and not runaways."

"See who is willing to go. In the meantime I will go talk to Osceola. He will have a plan," said Cowokoci.

"I will await your return, and we will go in together," John Horse said with assurance. With that, Cowokoci left to go to Osceola.

It was a short distance and Cowokoci arrived in time for a meal.

"Join me for some food" Osceola said to Cowokoci. Morning Dew, Osceola's wife recently reunited with him, served warm stew in bowls made from hollowed out gourds. She served fry bread made from coonti flour to soak up the liquid.

"This is good stew," said Cowokoci. "It has been a while since I've had hot food."

"Yes," replied Osceola. "This war has kept us on the run. Life has been hard." After they ate, Morning Dew removed the bowls and left the men to talk."

"Are you well?" asked Cowokoci.

"I have this fever," answered Osceola. "Curse the white man. It is his disease. He has ruined our land. He has ruined my life."

"Yes," agreed Cowokoci.

"I feel you are troubled. Is this about your father?" asked Osceola.

"Yes," answered Cowokoci. "He is held in the stone fort at St. Augustine. General Jesup has said he will hang him if I don't return and bring in the chiefs for a talk."

Osceola shook his head. He was quiet while he thought for a moment. *This fever is muddling my brain*, he thought. *This is not a time to be muddled.* After a few moments, he spoke. "Do you think this is a trick?"

"I do not trust General Jesup," said Cowokoci. "I do not trust any white man's words, but I must return for my father's sake."

"He is a great chief; his life is important," agreed Osceola.

"Thank you Osceola for your respect," Cowokoci said gratefully.

"I will come for a talk. Tell General Jesup I will be at Pellicer's Creek in three days," said Osceola. "But first let us make a plan."

Cowokoci shook his head in agreement. He leaned in closer to hear Osceola's wise words: "General Jesup will never release your father, and he will imprison you given the chance."

"I do know this," whispered Cowokoci.

"You Cowokoci are the strongest leader we have right now. I am sick. Your father is captured. Micanopy is fat and lazy," said Osceola.

"Abiaka is up for the fight," remarked Cowokoci.

"True, but he too is on in years. I think our best chance of winning your father's freedom is to have something the general must have back," said Osceola

"Something, or someone to trade?" asked Cowokoci.

"Exactly. I will wait at Pellicer's Creek," Osceola said. "I will bury my gun just beneath the sand at my feet. I will have my braves do the same. When the general or his representative comes to talk, we will capture him. Then we will trade for your father."

"This is our best plan I think," said Cowokoci.

"Yes. Have John Horse take in the slaves then come back here to be ready for the talk," ordered Osceola. "This will show our good intention to talk and end the war."

"Thank you." Cowokoci bid his friend good-bye and headed back to John Horse's camp where Cowokoci's brother and uncle waited with John Horse for his return.

"Thank you for coming uncle," Cowokoci said.

"My brother's life is at stake. I will do what I can," replied his uncle.

"Osceola has a good plan. We will appear unarmed at the talk, but our guns will be in the sand at our feet. We will take the general prisoner and trade for my father," said Cowokoci.

"Do you think this will work?" his brother asked.

"We will do our best to make it work," said Cowokoci. "Now we must go to St. Augustine."

John Horse spoke. "I have seventy-nine plantation slaves that want to go back. Slaves who are tired of life on the run, and who are hungry and fear capture anyway. We will surrender them as our 'captives' so they will not be punished for escaping the plantations."

"Hopefully that will satisfy General Jesup and show our good faith until we can gain the release of my father. Let us prepare to leave. We will meet with the General," said Cowokoci. "I will tell him John Horse has slaves to be returned and will be waiting with Osceola. We will return and hide in the woods and surround the soldiers. Osceola will take the commander hostage."

"What if he doesn't let you leave St. Augustine?" asked John Horse.

"I think he will," Cowokoci responded. "He wants Osceola the most. If he arrests me, then Osceola will disappear into the scrub and swamps."

Cowokoci led the entourage to meet General Jesup. The entire group followed him including his uncles.

Unfortunately for the Seminoles, General Jesup had his own plan. The talks were a ruse; Jesup intended to arrest every Seminole with or without cause. He was still smarting from the embarrassment of the encampment escape. He blamed Cowokoci and John Horse for causing him to lose face with Washington. This time he would be successful. This time his trick would work.

"General, the Seminoles are approaching the city," one guard shouted.

"Very good," said General Jesup. "Treat them as if they are guests. When they are secured in one place, surround them with the troops and arrest them."

"Yes sir. I will prepare the company," said the guard.

General Jesup went to greet the Seminole delegation. He shook Cowokoci's hand. "Welcome. I'm sure you will want to visit with your father. Come this way."

The delegation followed the general into the courtyard of Fort Marion. Emathla was sitting in the courtyard and rose to greet his sons.

"My sons. I am happy to see you. I'm not sure you should have come. I think this is a trap," whispered Emathla.

"Your life is all that is important at this moment," said Cowokoci.

As they were speaking, the gates to the fort were shut and locked. Army troops surrounded the delegation and quickly stripped the Indians of their weapons.

"General Jesup," said Cowokoci. "What is the meaning of this? We have come to talk peace. We are under the protection of your white flag. Do you not honor even your own laws?"

General Jesup stared at Cowokoci. He turned and left the fort. The General was not in a good mood. He hated capturing the Seminoles under such deceitful means, but he also had an obligation to the country to end this war. *It would not end with the war chiefs at large, and they have proven over and over again that they too practice deceitful ways*, he thought. *I must make amends for the Tampa Bay escape.*

As the Seminoles were being locked up in Fort Marion, General Hernandez was nearing the spot to meet Osceola. Osceola heard them approaching. The clicking of the horse's hooves on Old Kings Road announced the army was near. John Horse was there with the escaped enslaved Africans that wished to return to plantation life. They were hungry and tired of hiding. They feared capture by slave hunters and being separated from their families. The institution of slavery was vile, but to these broken men and women, it seemed inevitable. Returning on their terms was the only option they could conceive.

Hernandez approached Osceola and shook his hand. The chief stood under the white flag. He looked down the road and could see many soldiers. Too many, he thought, for a peace talk. It dawned on Osceola that he would not be taking Hernandez captive today, but instead he would be the captive.

The general did not look Osceola in the eye. "Why have you come?" he asked.

Osceola pointed to the white flag above his head and said, "We had a message from Emathla to make peace. I am here to make peace." Osceola could hear the crackling of twigs and the rustle of pine needles as the soldiers moved through the woods to surround the Indians.

"In the Council at Fort King, Coa Hadjo and your chiefs agreed to give up the slaves. Are you prepared to honor your agreement?" Hernandez stated without emotion.

Osceola was stunned. He never agreed to any such thing. Coa Hadjo, standing beside Osceola, denied any such agreement took place. It was clear to Osceola that this entire meeting was a ruse. General Hernandez was not directly speaking to Osceola. He was speaking General Jesup's words and not his own. The soldiers had dismounted and formed a complete ring around the camp. The Captain tipped his hat, and the soldiers seized everyone in sight. The Indians did not resist. It was not the Seminole way to engage in a battle that would end in certain death. Osceola was placed upon his horse and led to St. Augustine. His followers straggled behind. John Horse walked behind the others. He feared for his family and his future. He had his freedom papers, but would the general honor them? *I knew General Jesup was a snake with two tongues*, he thought as he walked. *He has not been honorable or honest in any way. He is a man of shame.*

Ironically, many of the citizens of the United States agreed with John Horse. Newspapers across the land decried the capture of the noble Osceola under the white flag. He was, after all, defending his land from invaders. He was only protecting his family. Congress debated the action, and General Jesup was forced to defend his actions. Jesup stated that he told the Indians to come in only if they intended to emigrate. Besides, they were fugitives since they escaped from Tampa Bay; therefore, he was arresting fleeing prisoners. In the end, the general did not face any charges. The Congress felt he was doing his job as best he could.

At the moment the general was feeling pretty confident. "Finally," said General Jesup to General Hernandez. "Finally, I have the major war chiefs locked up in an impenetrable fort. No one can escape from here."

"Yes sir," Hernandez responded. "You do have them secured. However, I did not feel good about taking Osceola under the white flag."

"I know. Neither did I," admitted Jesup, "but I also know it was the only way to capture him."

"Yes, I suppose. I pray we did the right thing," Hernandez conceded.

"To end this war is the right thing," Jesup declared.

Once again General Jesup informed Washington that the war effort was done. The only thing left to do was to negotiate the removal of the Seminoles remaining at large.

However John Horse and his companions had other ideas. They planned the impossible—an escape.

Thirty

For the next month, Washington negotiated with the remaining chiefs. Cherokee chiefs acted as emissaries; they were sent from Washington to negotiate peace talks. Micanopy went to Abiaka to talk before he met with Jesup.

"Micanopy, honored chief," said Abiaka. "Sit. My wife will bring food, drink. Then we talk."

Micanopy sat. They shared warm stew served in coconut bowls. Micanopy ate three helpings of fry bread. He loved fry bread most of all. Finally he spoke.

"Jesup wants us to talk at their Fort Melon next week," said Micanopy.

"I will not go," replied Abiaka adamantly. He crossed his arms on his chest.

"We have guarantees from Washington, brought to us by the Cherokee," assured Micanopy.

"Guarantees mean nothing," argued Abiaka. "Jesup has arrested Emathla, his sons and followers, John Horse, the great Osceola, and his family and followers all at supposed peace talks."

"The Cherokee guarantee our safety," insisted Micanopy. "They come straight from the great white chief in Washington. They speak for him. He rules General Jesup. I think it important that we all be there for the safety of our brethren that are locked up in the great fort in St. Augustine."

"It is a trick and he will capture you too," countered Abiaka.

"I don't think so. My people need rations. I will negotiate rations while pretending to prepare to leave," said Micanopy.

"You are a fool and I will not go," Abiaka maintained.

Micanopy nodded acceptance of Abiaka's decision. "I understand. As you wish."

The talks began at Fort Melon on December fifth. Micanopy, his remaining free chiefs, and thirty warriors arrived for the talks. Abiaka did not attend. Instead he went deeper into the Everglades. Abiaka predicted what would happen next.

"We have come in peace under the white flag," began Micanopy.

"Enough of these talks," replied General Jesup. "It is time to emigrate."

"We will agree, but we need time. Many of our people are scattered, and it will take time to gather them," said Micanopy.

"No more time," insisted General Jesup. "Asking for time is just a stall tactic. You have negotiated before with no intention of honoring our talks. All will surrender in ten days, and all here are held as hostages until that time."

The Cherokee delegation was shocked. They had come to negotiate believing the U.S. Government acted in good faith. Now it appears they were pawns in a diabolical plan to capture the Seminole. General Jesup used them to trick the Seminole.

"This is an outrage," said one of the Cherokee chiefs. "We came in good faith under the protection of your president."

"You may be under the protection of my government, but the Seminole are not," retorted General Jesup.

The Cherokee delegation was speechless. They left at once to protest in Washington.

General Jesup ordered Micanopy west to the Indian lands. The great chief wept as the ship carrying him and his followers set sail from Tampa Bay. When Abiaka heard of this treachery, he shook his head and thought about what a fool Micanopy was. He sent out runners to inform all free Seminole to move southward with no regard for peace as an option. He would be camped on the headwaters of the great Okeechobee lake. He asked for all to join him there. At this point he knew he must take over the tribe and keep the remaining Seminole free. He needed to know how many braves he had under his command. He ruled the Miccosukee, the most ruthless of the Seminole. They would fight to the death.

In the meantime the captives in Fort Marion had other plans. There was only one opening in the cell in which they were held. It was covered with two bars.

"We must escape," said John Horse.

"Yes, we must," said Cowokoci. "We will be free or die trying."

"I've been looking and measuring the window opening," said John Horse. "I think we can squeeze through it."

"I don't know. It looks awfully small," said Emathla. "What if you get stuck?"

"Then we died trying," said Cowokoci. Everyone laughed at his joke.

"We are all growing sick in this dark damp place," said Osceola. "I no longer have the physical strength to escape, so you Cowokoci and John Horse will have to escape for me and keep my vision of a free Seminole alive."

They both nodded an affirmative yes to Osceola's plea. "We can use sickness to our advantage," said John Horse. "We need the black drink to make us lean. Only at our smallest can we fit through that opening."

"I will tell the guards we need herbs for Osceola's fever," said Cowokoci. "If we drink it, we will grow thinner. It is a couple of weeks till the new moon. When the sky is darkest, we will leave. That is the right amount of time for the black drink to work and purge the poisons from our bodies."

"Assin-ye-o-la," said Osceola drawing out the last syllable just as he did in his coming of age ceremony. Osceola's name means black drink singer. He was noted for his singing during his purification ceremony. The black drink is made from the leaves of the Florida holly tree. The Seminole and other southeastern Indian tribes used the drink for purification rituals because it induced vomiting. The vomiting would cause the war chiefs to lose weight.

"I will tell the guards that I need the plants for medicine for my fever. They will allow our women out of the fort to pick it. They have very little concern of them escaping," said Osceola.

"This is a good plan. In the meantime we need to get up to the opening and make sure our heads will fit through," said Cowokaci.

"Yes," agreed John Horse. "If my head goes through, everything else will follow." Again everyone laughed at the small joke.

There was a guard stationed outside the door of the cell continually, but he was fat and lazy, and he often slept through his guard duty.

"Cowokoci!" said John Horse. "I hear him snoring. Let's try this."

"Yes," agreed Cowokoci. "In the meantime," he said to the braves, "cut up the bags that we sleep on and make ropes. Use the back of the bag that rests on the floor so the guards will not detect what is going on."

Then Cowokoci climbed onto John Horse's shoulders. He reached as far up the wall as he could and he worked a knife that one of the women smuggled into the cell into the crack between two of the massive stones that made the wall. He pushed the blade entirely into the wall so that only the handle was sticking out. John Horse held onto Cowokoci's ankles to help support him as he worked. It was an arduous job. He shifted his weight to maintain balance as Cowokoci struggled with the knife and wall. Finally it was in and secure.

"Throw up one of those ropes," Cowokaci whispered to his men. Just then the guard ceased snoring. Everyone froze. It seemed like forever, but after a few seconds the guard began snoring again. Everyone breathed a sigh of relief. If their plot was discovered, they all knew Jesup would order them to be put into chains. Then any hope of escape would be lost. Cowokoci threw the rope over one of the bars in the opening. It fell to the floor. Determined he tried again. This time he could not reach both ends of the rope. He tried again and again. Finally he held both ends of the rope in his hands. Using the rope, he scaled the wall up to the opening.

John Horse watched intently. It was very dark but he could see Cowokoci's outline in the moonlight that came through the opening. He worked his shoulders loosening the muscles that were taut from Cowokoci standing on them for so long. Soon his shoulders loosened and he relaxed. Cowokoci was now hanging from one of the bars in the opening while he worked loose the other one. The fort was old and the bars were rusty. It took several minutes, but finally Cowokoci held the bar in his hand.

Now for the real test. Would his head fit through the opening? Cowokoci maneuvered his body so that his head was next to the opening. Slowly he pushed his head into the window. It fit. It was tight, but it fit. Overjoyed he put the bar back into place and lowered himself onto the floor. John Horse grabbed his legs and helped to ease him down. A crash would awaken the guard.

"It fit!" whispered Cowokoci. "I can get my head through."

"Now we just need to make our bodies smaller," said John Horse. "The black drink will accomplish that!"

They allowed themselves a few moments of joy. Osceola watched from the corner. He was very sick. He knew he would never be able to escape. He knew his time as a warrior was nearly done. He took solace in the fact that his young followers would continue the war effort. He could be at peace knowing his dream of a free Seminole would continue with Cowokoci and John Horse. He would be with them in spirit; his spirit would continue to fuel the war effort.

The next day the women prepared the black drink. They were allowed in the courtyard during the day for sunshine and exercise. They placed Osceola on a blanket in the middle of the courtyard. They chanted over him while they drank the drink. For the next week the warriors drank the black drink. They vomited and vomited. They took in little food. They grew thinner by the hour. The U.S. Army medic came to see them. He listened to their stomachs. He measured their fevers. He decided they had the flu and just needed much water and rest. He never considered that the warriors were making themselves sick. It never occurred to him that the herbs they used for medicine were the cause.

Finally it was time.

"Three days hence will be the new moon. That is when we should go." said John Horse.

"Yes," agreed Cowokoci. "It will be darkest on that night. We will escape or die trying. I was made from the sands of Florida. I would rather die in Florida than live in Arkansas."

"I fear I would never make it to Arkansas. My family would be scattered to slavery. I could not live with that," said John Horse. Cowokoci shook his head in agreement. He understood his friend's concerns. He patted him on the shoulder to comfort him.

Three days later Osceola spoke. "My companions, it is time," he said. He looked at John Horse and Cowokoci. "You are my hope. You must carry on my dream. I am too sick to go. I would only slow you down and risk your capture. Go and be brave."

"Son," said Emathla to Cowokoci. "You are the chief now. Micanopy is old and sick. The future of our people rests with you. You are a strong leader. You will do what is right."

Cowokoci was humbled by his father's praise. "I will do my best. With my friend John Horse at my side we will be victorious."

"Go my son and be safe," said Emathla.

The guard outside the door was drinking and singing. He came into the cell to rouse the Indians. He wanted them to join him in his revelry. They pretended to be asleep.

"If he doesn't go away, we will tie him up and put a bag over his head so he does not rouse the entire fort," whispered Cowokoci. "We could never escape with everyone awake."

"If we fake sleep, maybe he will go away," replied John Horse. This they did, and it worked. The guard grew weary and left. Soon he was passed out snoring outside the cell.

Cowokoci went first. He stood atop John Horse's shoulders and once more drove the knife into the wall. He hoisted himself up. He tied one rope to the bar still in place in the window. He threw another rope outside so he could let himself down slowly. It was a fifty foot drop. He did not want to slip and break his neck attempting to escape. He put his head into the opening. It was a very tight fit, but he maneuvered inch by inch until he was looking at the outside. The stone walls pushed in on his body. He exhaled and propelled himself through the aperture. The opening was confining and the walls thick but he made it. If not for the rope he was holding, he would have plummeted to the ground head first. Soon he was standing outside the fort. His skin was scraped and he was bleeding slightly but he was free. He tugged the rope as a signal for the next man to come. Nocose Hadjo went next. He was nearly through the opening when he whispered, "I am stuck."

"Don't panic," instructed Cowokoci. "Push out all your breath and pull hard on the rope." This he did but he pulled a little too hard and fell to the ground. At first, Cowokoci thought he was dead. He dragged him to the moat where he splashed his face, and Nocose Hadjo revived.

"What happened?" Nocose Hadjo asked gasping for breath.

"You pulled too hard and fell to the ground. I thought you were dead," said Cowokoci.

"I'm fine and I'm free of the fort!" he laughed.

One by one the Seminoles crawled through the small opening in the inescapable Fort Marion. The Spanish built the fort from 1672 to 1696 to withstand cannon ball fire. It was constructed out of blocks of coquina with mortar made from oyster shells. Even after a hundred years the roughness of the coquina tore at Seminole flesh. Ignoring the physical pain of scraped and cut skin, one by one, they stood on free ground. John Horse was the last to come through. He was thin and had little trouble with the opening. Just as he landed on the ground, a noisy group of soldiers walked by.

The Seminole froze. No one moved or even breathed. The soldiers kept on walking. The dark night made the Seminoles invisible against the dark stones of the fort.

Once the danger passed, the warriors silently moved south. No one in the fort or the village detected anything. Two soldiers walking and talking passed within a few feet of Cowokoci, but they saw nothing. *The spirits of the ancestors have made us invisible*, he thought. The Indians made their way to the head of the Tomoka River where Cowokoci's followers were camped. When they arrived, the warriors were holding a council. They were arguing.

"We should go to the great lake and join Abiaka," one warrior declared.

"Or should we go to Arkansas and join Micanopy?" asked another.

"I think all the prisoners in the fort are dead," cried another. "We need to do what Cowokoci would want us to do which is to fight."

Just then Cowokoci and John Horse walked into the circle. The warriors were awestruck. Were these ghosts? Soon they realized their great leaders were in front of them and they laughed and cheered.

"My brothers," said Cowokoci. "General Jesup is treacherous. He can no longer be trusted. He captured all of us under his white flag of peace. My father and Osceola are still in his prison. They were too sick to escape."

"We escaped through a small window. We lost skin and blood but we gained freedom," said John Horse. "Now we must show the white man who this land really belongs to. We will fight and we will win."

The warriors cheered. One spoke, "Micanopy has been captured. He is on a boat that left Tampa. He wept as it pulled away. Abiaka is at the headwaters of Lake Okeechobee. He has asked that all free Seminole join him there."

"Then that is where we will go," said Cowokoci. The escaped prisoners ate heartily. They were hungry from starving themselves to better fit through the small opening in the fort. It was a joyous evening. "Tonight we relax; tomorrow we ride to Abiaka and prepare for war." He then dispatched a young brave to inform Abiaka that they would arrive tomorrow ready for battle.

Thirty-one

"What do you mean, they have escaped?" screamed General Jesup. He threw his papers onto his desk and stormed out of his office. The sergeant backed against the wall to give him wide berth as he ran to the cell that held the Seminole. General Jesup was furious. Once again he underestimated the war spirit and cleverness of the Seminole.

"Where are they?" General Jesup screamed.

Osceola and Emathla were sitting on the floor talking. Emathla pointed toward the opening. "They were tired of being locked up so they left."

"How?" retorted General Jesup. "How could they fit through that small opening?"

"See for yourself," said Osceola. "They left skin and blood, but they are gone."

The General was extremely agitated. He shook and fumed. Once again he assured Washington that he had things under control, and once again he must report that he does not. He glared at Osceola and stomped back to his office with Osceola's laugh haunting his ears.

"Send a dispatch to President Jackson," Jesup screamed to his orderly. "Tell him that the only end to this war will be in battle. Tell him there is no point in negotiating a peace treaty. The Seminole will not honor it anyway."

"Yes sir," said the orderly.

"Bring Powell and King Phillip to me," he demanded. He showed his true feelings by calling Osceola and Emathla by their English names. He did not honor them as Seminole chiefs.

"Yes sir," the orderly obeyed.

Both men walked into General Jesup's office with their heads held high. They were proud, but the toll the war has taken on them showed in their weakened bodies.

"I am very angry," said General Jesup. "Did I not treat you well as guests?"

"Since when do you lock up guests in a dark room?" asked Emathla. "Since when do you capture peaceful men under the white feather of peace?"

"That is not how you treat guests," said Osceola. "We were prisoners of war. It is every brave's duty to escape capture."

"I am proud of my sons," said Emathla. "They are men. They act like men."

General Jesup could not argue with their logic. It is every soldier's duty to escape the enemy. "How can we end this conflict?" asked General Jesup sounding helpless and desperate.

"We cannot," replied Osceola. "You cannot be trusted to honor peace talks; therefore, there are no more talks."

"So it is fight to the death?" Jesup asked.

"It is," responded Osceola. "I am sick. I can no longer fight. It is up to the young men now. The young men are determined."

"What if I put you to death in the courtyard for all to witness?!" demanded Jesup.

"Then we die proudly defending our people," said Emathla.

"That is what I thought your answer would be. I informed President Jackson of this," said General Jesup.

With that, the meeting was ended, and the prisoners returned to their cell.

At that very moment, Cowokoci and John Horse with their followers in tow, headed to meet up with Abiaka. When Cowokoci touched free ground outside of Fort Marion, it reaffirmed the Seminole spirit with him at the head of the tribe. With Micanopy on his way to the west and Emathla locked up with no hope of escape, Cowokoci was next in line. He was a ruthless warrior and a great leader. He never asked anything of his warriors that he, himself, would not do. He was smart and with John Horse at his side, he felt victory was inevitable. John Horse was also smart. He was an accurate shot and he could track at a gallop. He spoke several languages. He could read and write English, which came in very handy when dealing with captured soldiers. John Horse's followers had remained at large when John Horse was captured. Now they were all united and ready for war.

General Jesup considered the war spirit of the Seminole. He knew these next few months would not be easy. The Seminole were more determined than ever, so in response, he assembled more troops than at any other time. He had nearly nine thousand men at his disposal counting both active military and volunteer militias. The Seminole numbered five thousand with fifteen hundred of them warriors. The odds were greatly in favor of the United States, but would the climate and the terrain be enough to even up the odds?

Thirty-two

Abiaka welcomed Cowokoci and John Horse with food and drink. They sat in counsel planning their next move.

"I am very glad to see you free. I feared that General Jesup put you all to death," said Abiaka.

"Other than lying to us about the white flag and locking us up in a dark cell, he was cordial," said John Horse. "He treated us fairly well."

"Cordial?" asked Cowokoci. "Locking up free men is not cordial."

"True, true," replied John Horse, "But I mean he did not threaten us. He did not torture us."

"That is true, but he is a lying cheating man otherwise. The white man is greedy. He has broken all contracts made with us," Cowokoci remarked. "The military leaders are treacherous. They have allowed abduction of our family and friends. I am more determined than ever that I will defeat them. I will kill as many as I can physically accomplish."

"I will not disagree with that. And now we must plan," said John Horse. "General Jesup will be very angry, and he will pursue us with a vengeance."

"Yes," said Abiaka. "He will want revenge. I have camped here at the headwaters of this great lake because I think it is easily defendable."

"The many trees will serve as natural turrets for our best shooters," said John Horse.

"We should cut the grasses and the soldiers will take the easiest path. We can funnel them right to us," said Cowokoci.

"Very good idea," said John Horse. "I will have my men plant pointed stakes in the ground on this side of the swamps. If the soldiers make it this far and we end up in hand to hand combat, we can push them onto the hidden stakes and end their fight."

"I am not for hand to hand combat," said Abiaka. "I am old and I do not wish to engage in battle that will cost many Indian lives including my own."

"I agree," said John Horse. "But at this point, we need a decisive victory to make General Jesup and his chiefs in Washington understand that we are not defeated."

"You speak correctly John Horse," said Cowokoci. "Besides, as Abiaka said, we have the great lake to escape into if we become overwhelmed."

"I don't see that happening though," said John Horse. "This is the perfect place to engage the soldiers. Our sharpshooters can fell the men in the first line of the army with one volley."

"Exactly," said Cowokoci. "And they will be defenseless because our guns have a longer range."

"Stupid Americans," said Abiaka. "With all the money they have spent to drive us from our land, you would think they would buy the best rifles for their army."

"But the Spanish rifle is superior and the United States is not friends with the Spanish," said John Horse.

"Luckily for us," laughed Cowokoci. "This time we will be victorious. I will rid this land of the white man once and for all, or I will die doing it. It is up to the Creator." For such a ruthless fighter, Cowokoci was a very spiritual man.

Cowokoci had a twin sister who died. She appeared to him one night telling him of the peace she feels with the Creator. "It is very lovely here," she told him. She also told him he was not marked for an early death. For this reason, Cowokoci never feared a fight.

The men went to their followers with instructions for preparing the battlefield. Spies were sent out to track the soldiers' movements. The women prepared food bags for the braves that would wait in the trees. The Seminole would be fed and rested when a tired and worn-out army reached them.

"Come," called one Seminole woman to her children. "Let us move the canoes to the water and cover them with grasses."

"Why mamma?" asked her small daughter.

"So if our braves need to escape, they can uncover the canoes and be in the middle of the lake before the soldiers realize they left."

"Oh that is good," said the child. She ran to gather the grasses that the braves were cutting down to make a path for the soldiers. She passed her sister and stopped to watch for a moment. Her sister was grinding coonti root to make fry bread to feed the warriors. Everyone was busy. Gun powder was measured scrupulously to insure no waste. The proper amount was separated into small bags for quick reloading. Shot balls were shaved carefully to fit each rifle perfectly. Every detail was checked and rechecked to insure a quick and accurate first volley. The enemy would be badly wounded before they even realized they were upon the Seminole. The tribe worked in unison toward a common goal—defeating the invading enemy.

While the Seminoles planned and prepared, so did General Jesup.

"We now have more troops in Florida than at any other time," said Jesup to General Hernandez.

"Yes sir, we do," replied Hernandez. "According to my report, there are almost nine thousand troops at our disposal including almost two hundred friendly Indians. They will be a big help in tracking and finding the Seminole."

"I'm a little concerned with the militia. I have forty five hundred regular army and marines, but I can't seem to end the squabbles between the regular enlisted men and the volunteer militias," said General Jesup. Concern showed on his face.

"I think that is easily solved by keeping them separate," said Hernandez. "I will take the Florida Volunteers under my command. I am confident I can control them."

"I guess we will make it work. I want four columns moving southward at the same time. I want to trap the Seminole in the Everglades where we can surround, capture and destroy all of them. My intelligence reports say there are about five thousand Seminole but only about fifteen hundred warriors," said General Jesup.

"Fifteen hundred should be no problem for eight thousand soldiers," Hernandez assured the general.

"That is true," agreed General Jesup. "Let's get this war over with once and for all. I'm tired of this insect-infested swamp land that is valueless to anyone but our president. I cannot understand why Van Buren will not let this one go. I know it was a priority of Jackson, but I thought that would end when he left office."

"The southern slave-holders have a lot of clout in Washington. They have lost many slaves to the Seminole," Hernandez reasoned.

"I know, and for what we have spent on this war, we could have reimbursed every one of them tenfold," remarked General

Jesup. "Oh good, here come Colonels Taylor and Smith. I will now layout my plans for the final battle."

The colonels entered General Jesup's quarters. "Colonel Zackary Taylor and Colonel Smith reporting for duty, sir," announced Taylor.

"Welcome, gentlemen," said General Jesup. "At ease. Have a seat." General Jesup turned toward his orderly. "Bring these men some refreshments. I expect this to be a long meeting." The orderly left the tent to fetch food and drink.

"As I was telling General Hernandez here, I want a four pronged attack. I want to force the Seminole southward and trap them in the Everglades." The colonels listened intently. "Hernandez will command the Florida Volunteers. He will move south from St. Augustine and march along the eastern side of the St. John's River. General Eustis, who is at Fort Mellon, will leave there and move along the western side of the St. John's River."

"This is a good plan, General Jesup," said Colonel Taylor.

"Yes, I believe it is. I want you, sir, to move southeasterly from Tampa Bay to the Kissimmee River. Establish a fort on the Kissimmee River as a supply depot, and then move toward Lake Okeechobee."

"Yes, sir," Taylor responded.

"Colonel Smith, I understand your Louisiana Volunteers are holding the territory south and east of Lake Okeechobee," said Jesup.

"Yes sir, that is true," said Smith.

"Good," Jesup proclaimed. "Maintain that position and move some troops toward the lake. This will force the Indians to move together near the lake where I intend to trap them."

The commanders listened as General Jesup explained. "I want this to be the final battle. I want to once and for all end this conflict. We outnumber the Seminoles almost eight to one. Gentlemen, you have your orders. Let us have no mistakes. We must be victorious this time."

The Generals were confident. They liked the plan and they were sure they could execute it. With all the confidence of the U.S. Government behind them, they would make this plan work. What they didn't know is that the Seminoles knew their every move and were preparing for a victorious battle themselves. General Jesup underestimated the Seminole twice before, he was determined that would not happen this time.

Back at the big lake, John Horse spoke. "We need to send out decoys to make sure the soldiers come from the direction we choose so our sharpshooters can pick them off from the best angle."

"Let us tax the white soldiers even more. Let us send woman and children to surrender. They will eat up their food and slow down the progression of the march," added Cowokoci.

"Good idea," agreed John Horse. He turned to his sister's husband. "Brother-in-law," he said, "Will you sit on the path and await capture so you can send the soldiers in our direction?"

"I can do that," replied the brother-in-law.

"Once you do, escape and join the battle from this side," John Horse directed.

"I will do my best," he said.

"Very good. I think we are nearly ready. Let us meet for one final talk and then we will fight. My spies tell me that Colonel Zachary Taylor is at Fort Gardner near the Kissimmee River. He has a thousand men and he is preparing to leave the fort in search of us," said John Horse.

"Then let them come. I am ready," said Cowokoci. "I have never been more ready in my life." They clasped hands in a gesture of solidarity, a small release of emotion rarely seen in Indians. The chiefs met in a council circle. No one spoke while the women served enough food and drink to fill them up. Once satiated, Cowokoci spoke first.

"My friend, John Horse has sent his brother-in-law to be captured by the white soldier chief Taylor so he can send him our way. He has many soldiers with him; however, they march in a straight line so they are easily picked off by our sharpshooters."

"Your brother-in-law is a brave and honorable Seminole," said Abiaka.

"Yes, he is clever, and I think he will be safe," said John Horse.

"The women and children will be moved south along the west side of the lake for their protection," said Cowokoci. "They have prepared the powder and shot. Each warrior will have a supply in their pouches. Young braves will run back and forth between the battle and the women's hiding place to re-supply the warriors as needed."

"The trees are notched to hold our guns so the sharpshooters will be accurate," added John Horse. "Each warrior has prepared his tree to suit his needs best. Also, we have sent several women and children to be captured along the way so they can send the soldiers in our direction."

"Everything is in place. We are greatly outnumbered but we have the advantage," said Cowokoci.

"Yes," agreed Abiaka. "We also have the lake behind us for safety. The soldiers cannot follow us into the lake."

"That is true," said John Horse. "Besides by the time we may be ready to escape south, I expect many of the soldiers will be wounded or dead. This will certainly turn them back because they always take their wounded with them and they always bury their dead. And remember, the white soldiers fight by orders. Shoot the officers first, and the ranks will be confused."

"Yes," said Cowokoci. "Indians fight as individuals. If our chief falls, we still know what to do. The white soldiers do not seem to know what to do when they lose their leader."

The Seminoles were satisfied with their preparations. All that was left to do was to await the arrival of the soldiers. They were grossly outnumbered—roughly three to one, and yet they were confident. All the resources of the Florida Indians were now concentrated in this one place for this one battle. The Seminole and Miccosukee warriors were commanded by the best leaders still in the field—Halpatter Tustenugee, Abiaka, Cowokoci, Halleck Tustenugee, and John Horse. They all fought a common enemy. Some fought for land, and some fought for freedom. John Horse would never see his family made into slaves for the white man. He would fight to the death, but more importantly he would fight smart and survive.

Colonel Zachary Taylor completed his preparations. He was ready to leave Fort Gardiner in search of the Seminoles.

"Inform the troops that we will leave at daybreak tomorrow," said Colonel Taylor.

"Yes sir, I will inform the officers promptly," his orderly responded.

The next morning, Colonel Taylor left Fort Gardiner with over a thousand men. When the troops were fifteen miles north of Lake Okeechobee, he ordered them to camp. While there, they built an advance depot to make moving supplies easier and timelier for the army. Colonel Taylor was resting in his tent when an officer appeared at the door.

"Sir, there is a Seminole here to see you," the officer announced.

"Is he alone? Send him in," said Colonel Taylor.

"Yes sir, he is alone," said the officer.

Ote Emathla entered the colonel's tent. "I am Ote Emathla. I am weary of war. I wish to turn myself in to you. I have sixty followers just outside camp who wish to come in also."

"Excellent," said Colonel Taylor. He was beaming as he stood to shake Ote Emathla's hand. "This is a smart decision. Get your people. They must be hungry. I will order rations for you and your people." Ote Emathla left the tent to gather his people.

"This is a good omen," said Colonel Taylor. "I think the Seminoles are ready to emigrate. They are as weary of war as we are."

"That is good news, sir. I will order them to follow the troops as we move south," said a lieutenant.

The next day, Colonel Taylor moved toward Lake Okeechobee. Along the way, he encountered stragglers from the Seminoles who surrendered to him and pointed toward the lake where he would find the Seminoles. Taylor was confident, yet he didn't know how ready they were to fight.

The Seminole's were all in a wooded patch above the swamp awaiting the army's arrival. Some were hidden in the tall grasses and many were in the trees giving them an advantage over a marching army. In front of the trees was an open bog with knee deep mud and five foot saw grass. It was three-quarters of a mile wide. The soldiers would have to traverse this bog to reach the Seminoles. Crossing would be difficult for the army. The Seminoles knew Taylor was close because they had been tracking him since he left Fort Gardiner.

"Here they come," said John Horse. He was perched in a tree. Cowokoci was beneath him behind a lightening charred tree stump.

"Have they started across the bog yet?" asked Cowokoci.

"No. They are hesitating," answered John Horse.

Cowokoci stepped from behind the tree and yelled to his followers: "Mill about so the soldiers will see us and come this way." He watched as Indians came out of hiding. "Good. Now pretend to notice them and duck so they think they discovered us by accident."

Abiaka spoke to the Miccosukee and told them to do the same. This they did and the soldiers saw them.

"Sir, there they are," reported Colonel Gentry who commanded the Missouri Volunteers. "They are hidden in those trees." The soldiers stirred at the sight of the Seminole. They were excited and nervous at the same time.

"I see that," replied Colonel Taylor.

"I think we should divide and encircle the Indians," said Gentry. They will have no escape route; the lake will trap them."

"I don't think this will be a very difficult operation. I think a frontal assault will be best. I do not want to divide the troops. Colonel Gentry, take your militia and lead the attack," responded Colonel Taylor.

"Yes, sir," replied Colonel Gentry. Although he didn't feel good about Colonel Taylor's order to proceed forward. He wanted to flank the Seminole from the other side.

While the soldiers struggled through the mud and water, the Seminoles watched. They saw the saw grass cut which frustrated the soldiers. The mud sucked at the soldiers boots. The struggle was intensified by holding their weapons out of the water. No soldier wanted to encounter an Indian without a working gun. The Seminole waited patiently while the soldiers made their way to the open field they had prepared adjacent to the bog. For all the soldiers knew, the few Indians they had seen had fled and they would find an empty camp when they reached the other side.

Finally by twelve-thirty in the afternoon, the Missouri Volunteers came from the water and were finally standing on solid ground. They relaxed a little. There were no Indians in sight. Just as they were collecting themselves to prepare for a charge, a piercing war cry was heard from the Seminole ranks. Just one hundred yards from the soldiers, gun shots rang from every tree and from behind every stump. Twenty-six men fell dead immediately including Colonel Gentry. He had followed orders pushing forward with a frontal attack, and he paid the highest price for it.

"The Colonel is down," yelled one Missouri Volunteer. As men dropped like flies, the volunteers panicked. They fled every which way but mostly back into the mud. They tried to reload amid all the panic. The Sixth Infantry was close behind. They tried in vain to locate the enemy; however, the Indians were concealed and difficult to see.

"Where are they? Can anybody locate them?" screamed one captain.

"Charge the trees," answered one soldier. "That is where they are."

Finally, the Sixth Infantry came out of the mud. Again, the Seminoles opened fire. Soldier casualties rose. By the time Colonel Taylor and the Fourth Infantry following the others, entered the fight, most of the officers were dead or wounded. During this melee the surrendered Seminoles all fled to the safety of the tribe. Colonel Taylor was left with no prisoners. The battle continued. Most of the soldiers fought bravely. Some hid in the bog for cover. The brave ones were cut down by Seminole fire. By three o'clock in the afternoon, the battle was over. The Seminole fled into the lake leaving Colonel Taylor demoralized and traumatized.

"Do you have a casualty report?" he asked of his one remaining alive officer.

"Yes sir. By my count, we have twenty-six dead but one hundred and twelve wounded. Most very badly wounded. Some won't live long. It will be difficult to transport them back through this bog."

"Nevertheless it must be done. Where are the prisoners?" asked Colonel Taylor.

"They are nowhere to be found," replied the officer.

Colonel Taylor shook his head. Maybe he should have followed Colonel Gentry's suggestion to surround the Seminole. *But the truth was*, he thought, *they were ready for us. It wouldn't have mattered from what direction we came.*

"Round up the cattle and horses," he ordered. The Indians had left their cattle and horses grazing and roaming in an adjacent field to make it look like the Seminole were surprised by the army's arrival. They wanted the soldiers to be surprised and walk into their trap so they could inflict the most casualties possible. Their plan worked. For all intents and purposes, the Second Seminole War was over.

The Epilogue

Colonel Zachary Taylor, who later became President of the United States, used the fact that he took the Seminole's horses and cattle as evidence that he won the Battle of Okeechobee. The divide between the volunteer militias and the army regulars was already great. They fought and bickered among themselves. Taylor exacerbated the problem by sending in the Missouri Volunteer Militia as the front guard while his own company followed in last. This was highly criticized; however, Taylor had friends in powerful places in Washington, D.C. so he was proclaimed a war hero and the victor instead of a commander who sacrificed volunteers for the safety of himself and his regular army.

The Seminoles and General Jesup knew differently. The Seminoles lost eleven warriors on that day and had only fourteen wounded. Abiaka took the Miccosukee and headed down the western shore of Lake Okeechobee. He settled deep in the southern Everglades where their descendants still live today. The Seminole headed south and east and fought two more battles at Loxahatchee River and Jupiter Inlet. They were victorious and even General Jesup was wounded at the Loxahatchee River. He was shot in the cheek and his glasses were broken. Had he not turned his head at the right moment, he would have been shot in the head and killed. It was not a serious wound, but he knew there was no winning of this war by the U.S. Army. He knew that as long as the Black Seminoles and the red Seminoles were united, there would be no end to these skirmishes. So Jesup made a bold move; he offered freedom to any Black Seminole willing to emigrate. This became known as Jesup's Proclamation. It was debated and ultimately decided that freedom could be granted under a treaty for peace. John Quincy Adams argued for this idea in Congress.

"By war the slave may emancipate himself; it may become necessary for the master to recognize his emancipation by a treaty of peace." he wrote.

Could John Horse believe these words? His closest ally, Cowokoci would not surrender under any circumstances, but for John Horse, his motivation for war was freedom for his people.

His dream was realized.

On April fourth eighteen thirty eight, John Horse arrived at Fort Bassinger with twenty-seven followers and surrendered to General Zackary Taylor. His life took many turns after that. He emigrated west, but soon returned to interpret for the U.S. Military in Florida. The war dragged on with no major events but there were still several war chiefs at large. John Horse was surely in contact with his old friend Cowokoci during this period, and negotiated Cowokoci's surrender at Fort Pierce in March of eighteen forty-one. Eventually both he and Cowokoci jointly took their people west.

At this point, Cowokoci probably gave up because he expected to be elected Head Chief of the Seminole in the west, but things did not go well. He lost the election to John Jumper. John Jumper was not sympathetic to the Black Seminoles and saw them as a potential revenue source. Problems in the Indian camps forced John Horse to take his people, leave in the night, and settle in Mexico. Cowokoci joined him. There they were given land and honors for their heroic deeds in defending the Mexican frontier from Native American marauders.

The Black Seminole descendants still reside in northern Mexico today where they enjoy the freedom that John Horse dedicated his life to achieving. John Horse died on August tenth in the year eighteen eighty-two when he was in Mexico City negotiating with the Mexican government for the land his people now own. On September twenty-first, nineteen thirty-eight, Mexican President Lazaro Cardenas signed a degree that was published in the Diario Oficial of November thirtieth, nineteen thirty-eight ratifying the original grant and extra land. John Horse, the original freedom fighter, had finally won his fight. His people now firmly owned the Nacimiento land. His legacy of freedom lives on. His leadership and fight that led to Jesup's Proclamation became the precedent for President Abraham Lincoln to free the slaves in the Emancipation Proclamation January first, eighteen sixty-three. He stated "that all persons held as slaves," within the rebellious areas, "are, and henceforward shall be free."

Turso

Notes:
1. Chapter 8—John Horse's marriage—John Horse was married to Susan, daughter of July, but at a much later date. There is evidence that he had a wife in these days, but her name, fate, and any details of this union are lost to history.

2. Chapter 11—Mary Godfrey reported this incident; however it is not likely that it was John Horse that she encountered. The name of the magnanimous Indian is lost to history.

3. Chapter 12—The taking of Osceola's wife, Morning Dew, is open for conjecture. Some sources say it certainly happened. It would give reason to Osceola's anger and bitterness toward the white men that were once his friends. Other sources claim it was a story made-up by the Abolitionists to spur anger against the slave-holders.

ABOUT THE AUTHOR

A love for Florida's young people and a passion for writing and exploring local history inspired Betty Turso, an English teacher at John I. Leonard High School in south Florida to pen her first historical novel, *John Horse: Florida's First Freedom Fighter*. In 2015 she received the President's Silver Medal Award for her book, *John Horse*, from the Florida Authors and Publishers Association. Ms. Turso currently lives in Lake Worth, Florida where she has resided since 1970. She attended Palm Beach State College and Florida Atlantic University. She earned a Master's degree in English, and she completed post-graduate work in creative writing at Florida International University. She was awarded National Board Teacher Certification in Adult and Young Adult English Language Arts in 2000 and in 2010. Ms. Turso enjoys writing about Florida's incredibly colorful and largely unknown past.

John Horse

Made in the USA
Columbia, SC
28 December 2018